W9-DBD-739

MULLIGAN GIRL

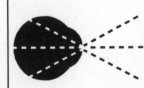

This Large Print Book carries the
Seal of Approval of N.A.V.H.

MULLIGAN GIRL

REBECCA L. BOSCHEE

THORNDIKE PRESS
A part of Gale, Cengage Learning

GALE
CENGAGE Learning

Detroit • New York • San Francisco • New Haven, Conn • Waterville, Maine • London

GALE
CENGAGE Learning™

Copyright © 2010 by Rebecca L. Boschee.
Thorndike Press, a part of Gale, Cengage Learning.

LIBRARY OF CONGRESS CATALOGING-IN-PUBLICATION DATA

Boschee, Rebecca L.
  Mulligan girl / by Rebecca L. Boschee.
    p. cm. — (Thorndike Press large print gentle romance)
  ISBN-13: 978-1-4104-2920-9
  ISBN-10: 1-4104-2920-2
  1. Chick lit. 2. Golf stories. 3. Large type books. I. Title.
PS3602.O833M85 2010b
813'.6—dc22   2010020899

Published in 2010 by arrangement with Thomas Bouregy & Co., Inc.

Printed in the United States of America
1 2 3 4 5 6 7 14 13 12 11 10

For CDB and AKB. Thank you for believing in me and for tolerating the dust bunnies.

CHAPTER ONE
ASSESSOR

I watched without astonishment as the composed sales professional appraised the pitifully scuffed bottoms of my fawn-colored, python skin, Ferragamo slingbacks.

Without a second glance, she held my platinum charge card between two perfectly polished fingers and swiped it to credit back my $637.99. She smiled sincerely as she handed back the card. "Thank you for your business, Mrs. Edwards. I'm sorry those didn't work out for you, but I hope that you can find time to shop with us some more today. We're having a sale on handbags."

"Not today, but don't worry . . . I'll be back." I smiled brightly at her, then turned toward the exit of the store. I stopped at a plush, cushioned bench near a live pianist to tap some preliminary notes into my BlackBerry: *September 3, 2:30 P.M.: Returned Salvadore Ferragamos to Nordstrom's after night of heavy dancing (House of Blues).*

Service experience: Exceptional (as usual).

My boss probably didn't need to know the part about the House of Blues, but I believed in providing details. Besides, I had to justify the cost of the first-class ticket from Sky Harbor to Midway, and the House of Blues was the perfect alibi. I flipped off the BlackBerry; I could finish the rest on my laptop when I got home. When I looked up from my task, I saw Mo walking toward me with an adorable, shabby-chic handbag tucked under her arm.

"*You* have to get this one, Ren. It practically leapt off the display and begged me to convince you to buy it."

"You could always buy it, you know," I told her. "Last I heard, Kane was doing pretty well."

"True, but he plays a lot of golf — that doesn't leave much left over for overpriced accessories, even if they are of the best quality."

I shook my head and smiled. "Sorry. I'm off duty for the day. Maybe tomorrow after my appointment at Red Door."

"You poor overworked little thing," Mo drawled.

"Now that isn't fair . . . I'm hardly little," I countered, purposely ignoring her good-natured barb about my job.

For the last four years I've had a job working for Affluence Index, Inc., as a customer experience assessor. Essentially, I get to pretend that I am one of America's elite, but not *too* elite. When I'm working, I am part of the most underserved demographic: the top ten percent of the wealthiest people in the United States, with a net worth of $3.1 million and an annual income of $256,000. My company measures and reports on the affluent customer experience by sending us into best-in-world businesses to pose as customers to experience and evaluate service. Three days a week, I'm Mrs. Edwards, customer extraordinaire, who flits from coffee at Starbucks to shopping at Nordstrom's to lunch at the latest haute bistro, all courtesy of my company-paid platinum charge card. The other two days I work in the office or at home entering data and benchmarking service experiences. My kind and I own seventy percent of all wealth in my country . . . on paper. Off paper I'm just Ren Edwards, named by my eccentric, artist mother after her favorite red oil paint, Alizarin Crimson, which was shortened and misspelled to Ren. My seventy-some-thousand income isn't bad for a single girl living alone in Arizona, even if it is Scottsdale, but it's those perks that really keep me going.

I stood up to my full five foot ten and looped my arm through Mo's, urging her toward the door. "Come on, I need to get home early tonight — big day tomorrow."

"Need a wake-up call?" Mo asked.

"Yes, you can come," I answered, then wrested the handbag away from her and plunked it onto the nearest countertop.

"You won't be making any more returns tomorrow, will you? It's so much more fun when we get to spend the money," Mo asked.

I laughed. The only real catch to my job is that it's to experience service, not goods, so all that stunning Baccarat glassware and those heavenly Salvatore Ferragamos do eventually need to be returned, with the aim of measuring that return service as part of the beginning-to-end experience.

"Nope, tomorrow's all about spending money. *Big* money."

"Then you can count me in." Mo was always game for just about anything. Her real name is Mary Jo Stemple, but that's way too stuffy for her personality. We've been best friends since college, where we were forced to share a dormitory suite with two girls who partied so much and had so many strange late-night visitors that they

10

ended up flunking every class scheduled before noon. Mo and I bonded out of necessity and have been inseparable ever since.

After college, I moved to Arizona, the warmest place I could think of, and Mo stayed in Wisconsin and married her high school sweetheart, Kane. No time or distance could dim the beam of our friendship, though, and eventually Mo and Kane moved out to Scottsdale, where they currently live in a sprawling ranch home only two streets over from my condo. Our friendship is that strong. I keep telling myself that their move had very little to do with Kane's love for golfing and his required job transfer.

"Don't look so smug," I said.

Mo clasped her hand to her chest and feigned an innocent look. *"Moi?"*

"Yes, you. This purchase isn't in the company budget, and I don't plan on returning it."

"So?"

"So, this one is going to end up costing you too."

"You can't scare me off with sweet talk. I'll be there at eight," she said.

I found Mo knocking on my door at promptly 8:00 A.M. Either she was as excited about my purchase as I was, or she

11

was quickly tiring of lying by the pool every morning. Either way, after two knocks she let herself in with a key. I was still buried under two inches of down comforter, and I swiftly covered my head and burrowed in deeper when I heard the door click.

"Wakey, wakey . . . . It's another beautiful day in the land of beautiful people!" I could hear her slightly nasally voice sing. "Oh, for goodness' sake, Ren, are you kidding me with that comforter? It's still a hundred and six degrees outside!"

That was a quirk of mine that Mo, being more recently transplanted from Wisconsin and still with "thick" blood, could not understand. I loved to crank my air-conditioning down to seventy-two and snuggle under the thick bedding, even in September. I flipped over to put my back toward her and groaned something unintelligible.

"Come on, sunshine, your appointment is at nine A.M. all the way over in Carefree — no time to dawdle today."

My new-car appointment. The car of my dreams was a two-year-old, mint-condition black Audi S4 Quattro with less than five thousand miles on it. I'm not sure which part of the equation I was more tickled with . . . the four-wheel drive, the low mileage or the inconspicuous three hundred and forty horsepower lurking under the hood. Mo's husband found it advertised in the local *Auto Trader* magazine and had already arranged an appointment for me before anyone else could snap it up. I think Mo's husband would make an excellent concierge, he's so thoughtful, but Mo says he actually kind of likes the grind of bioengineering.

"Ren?" She snatched the comforter off the bed, and I felt the air-conditioning drift over my bare legs and cause my skin to pucker with goose bumps.

"I ended up working late last night," I protest, trying unsuccessfully to snuggle under a single layer of sheets.

"Uh-huh, honey, you forget I know what kind of work you do. What? Were you kept up late by some tight-bunned bartender at the La-Di-Da Resort? And if so, by the way, why didn't you call me?"

"No, I was analyzing data!" I try to say in my most indignant, supercilious customer voice, but it comes out all early-morning froggy in my throat.

"Okay then, I'll hit Starbucks all by myself and come back for you."

That, as she knew it would, got my attention. I don't smoke and I drink only moderately, but the finely roasted, perfectly ground coffee bean is my one true vice. There was a time in my life when I visited Starbucks no less than three times a day, and they knew my name and purchasing habits better than my credit card company did. I was now down to once per day (okay, twice on some of those really rough days), and it was the number one driving thought that could get me out of bed in the morning.

Forty minutes later, with half of my nonfat latte coursing nicely through my veins, and Mo driving with one hand on the wheel of my six-year-old Volvo (which was soon to be hers) and the other on a bazillion-calorie Macchiato, we soared up Scottsdale Road toward Carefree. Another twenty-five minutes and we pulled into the long driveway of a huge, ranch-style home with a panoramic view of the nearby mountains.

A man with salt-and-pepper hair and wearing a polo shirt and Bermuda shorts appeared from around the back of the house.

"Hello there! Here to steal away my dream car, are you?"

I smiled at the man. He looked like the type to have taken very good care of my car over the past two years.

"Hi. I'm Ren Edwards. I'm very excited

to see the car . . . I can't believe it has so few miles." I stuck out my hand for him to shake.

He gripped my hand and gave it a hearty pump.

"Sure a little thing like you can handle a car like this? It's not your mother's Volvo, you know." The corner of his eyes crinkled warmly as he eyed my pearl-white Volvo. I laughed. At five foot ten, I had rarely been called little. I wondered if he knew how close to the mark his other comment was, though. My mother *had* sold me her car when I'd moved here from Wisconsin, and I've been driving it ever since. I couldn't wait to get into something a little less . . . domestic.

"Oh, I think I can handle it."

The man reached into his pocket for a garage door opener and clicked open one of the stalls of his four-car garage. A blast of cool air hit us in the face. An air-conditioned garage in Arizona — what a luxury! The man motioned for us to step aside so that he could back the car out; then he handed me a single key fob that flipped open like a jackknife.

I looked at Mo. She was eyeing the car suspiciously, looking for flaws.

There were none. This beauty was all

black, with black leather seats and dark, ceramic-tinted windows. It was in perfect condition.

I slipped behind the wheel and settled comfortably into the sculpted seat. I breathed in the faint scent of clean leather.

"You two take it out. I'll wait for you here," the man said. He must have sensed that for a young woman to conduct a true test drive she needed to have her best friend sitting shotgun while blasting the radio far louder than necessary. Smart man. Mo complied by hopping into the passenger seat and buckling up.

I popped up the tinted moon roof despite the heat, and I cranked on the engine. I paused for a second to savor the sound. It had a low, sexy growl. I smiled sideways at Mo. She looked a little nervous. I backed the car out of the drive and eased it out of the elite, little subdivision to Carefree Highway, where I punched the gas and ripped around the corner to test the swivel.

There was no swivel. The four wheels gripped the pavement like a lover and sent me soaring out onto open highway. Have you heard of the giggle factor? This car had the giggle factor times ten. No, times a hundred. I couldn't stop grinning as I accelerated over the curvy road that wound

16

through the foothills. I hadn't taken it more than two miles before I knew that this car and I were a match made in heaven.

"Mo," I said, flashing my pearly whites, "I believe you've got yourself a Volvo."

Thirty minutes later and thirty-two thousand dollars lighter, Mo and I drove side by side down Carefree Highway toward Scottsdale, a permanent grin etched on my face and ABBA blasting through my moonroof. If I had been passively looking for true love for the last few years, I had no idea I had been looking in the wrong place all that time.

Since this was a day to celebrate, I detoured for a celebratory coffee at Starbucks (it was too early for margaritas). I inched my way up the drive-through lane, careful to avoid the red curb in front of the window that could scratch my rims. The guy who took my order was new, I noted. He didn't use my name and didn't know my usual order. I was thinking that I might have to chalk this one down to a ho-hum customer experience when I heard his voice, very excited, as I pulled up.

"Wow! A three hundred and twenty horsepower, 4.2 liter V8 Audi S4. I want one of those when *I* grow up!"

"Three hundred and *forty* horsepower," I

corrected with a goofy grin. I accepted my latte and gave the guy a five-dollar tip. It was his first day, after all — so I should probably cut him a bit of slack.

Mo met me back at my condo. She must have called Kane on her cell because he was already in my parking lot, kicking at my tires.

"How much did you say you wanted for it?" he asked.

"Eight grand?" I suggested tentatively. That was the Blue Book trade-in. "I know I could probably get a bit more . . . but you guys are friends."

Mo looked at him hopefully. He nodded and walked to his truck to grab his checkbook. All in all, it was a very productive day for being well before noon.

"What else is on the agenda for today?" Mo asked me. "Kane is golfing with some buddies at one, so I'm free all day."

"He's golfing in this heat?" I ask.

"The green fees are only low for another few weeks and then they jump up to around two hundred dollars for eighteen holes. He doesn't mind the heat so much."

"That gives me an idea. I'm supposed to be thinking of an anniversary present for my husband and I need something I can purchase online. Maybe I'll get him a golf certificate. That would be really thoughtful of me."

"You're married now?"

"Oh yeah, didn't you know? I'm *Mrs.* Edwards. I've been married for years. In fact, this is my fifth anniversary — a milestone. You and Kane would really like him. He's a golfer."

"Yeah, only that lucky sap is probably going to get a primo round of golf during high season, isn't he?"

"Nothing but the best for my sweetie."

"Any godchildren I should know about?"

"Not yet, but you'll be the first to know. I've got my eye on a twelve-hundred-dollar Louis Vuitton diaper bag."

Mo rolled her eyes. "And I thought you'd never use that degree in art appreciation."

After Kane had replenished my savings account with at least a portion of its funds, Mo followed me up my steps and into my condo.

"You know, for being one of the wealthiest Americans, you don't live all that lavishly," she said.

"Yeah, unfortunately for me, most of those premium businesses eventually take back their goods after varying degrees of convincing."

"I see you couldn't convince someone to

take back this quilted Burberry shoulder bag."

"Yeah, truth is I didn't try very hard on that one. But I'm planning to try again as soon as buckled bags go out of style. I might even try taking that one back to one of their competitors. That would be really telling."

"Uh-huh."

I flipped open the laptop that sat atop my kitchen bar and waited for it to power on. "What's the name of the course that Kane goes to?" I called out.

"Desert Glow, or Desert Heat, or something like that. Desert Something."

"Found it. It's the resort right up the road, isn't it? Five stars — this should be good. Hey, Mo, do you know how much Kane is spending to golf even *off*-season? I don't think you'd like it," I said when I saw that the off-season price was around one hundred and fifty dollars per person and the peak season price was closer to three hundred dollars.

"You'd better not tell me. He just bought me a car, after all, and I have big plans for later tonight . . . I'd hate to spoil them."

I laughed. Mo often went along with the what-you-don't-know-won't-hurt-you philosophy. Me, not so much — but then again, I'd never been married, happily or otherwise. Maybe the secret was to not ask too many questions.

"Darn, the most I can buy a certificate for online is five hundred dollars. Start think-ing of something else I could buy."

"If I were you, I'd go with the five hun-dred. It's symbolic for the five blissful years you've been married. Then I'd spend a load on lingerie and call it a happy anniversary."

Not a bad idea, I thought . . . though lingerie was difficult to return after having been worn, thank God. It was a splendid idea, actually. I made a note in my Black-Berry to stop at Neiman's on my way back from the Red Door. I pressed Submit on my golf order and made some notes about the ease of use of the Web site, then checked my e-mail to see if they had sent confirma-tion and what the messaging looked like. It stated that my order would be processed within seventy-two hours, but I had paid extra for overnight express mail. Not a great start. We'd have to see how they did on fulfillment.

About two hours later, as Mo and I were sipping iced tea and reading in chaise lounges on my shaded balcony, the phone rang. I put down my novel, *Pride and Preju-dice,* which I was reading for about the fifth time, and answered it. The caller I.D. read

UNKNOWN CALLER.

"Mrs. Edwards?" an unfamiliar voice asked.

"Yes?" I cringed. I hated telemarketers, but allowed them to engage me since I could sometimes add bonus material to my research depending on who they represented.

"I'm Mark calling from Desert Fire Golf Course. I wanted to let you know that I received and am processing your online order. I plan to have the certificate sent out to you tomorrow by overnight mail."

Wow, personalized confirmation. They might actually redeem themselves.

"Okay, thanks. I appreciate your call."

"And, Mrs. Edwards?"

"Yes?"

"I see that you have frequented our spa in the past . . ."

Oh boy, here comes the sales pitch.

"I just wanted to let you know how much we appreciate your repeat business."

Wow again.

"Okay, well, thanks," I say, careful not to let myself sound too impressed.

"Have a great afternoon."

I hung up and entered some new timed, dated notes in a spreadsheet.

"Who was that?" Mo doesn't hesitate to

ask, looking up from her *Vogue*.

"Just the hubby, calling to let me know he'll be home late for dinner." I smiled. Confidentiality is confidentiality, and first and foremost, I am a professional, after all.

Chapter Two
COMPENSATION

Early Wednesday afternoon, driving home from my personal color consultation with six hundred dollars of cosmetics tucked cozily behind the seat, I threw the car into Sport and accelerated up the outside lane of the on-ramp to the freeway. I blew past two white Dodge Rams and an Audi A4 with ease. I gave the A4 a friendly little wave in my rearview mirror — really, they didn't know what they were missing. I loved freeway driving at this time of day . . . light traffic, blue skies, open road. It was too bad my exit came up so soon.

I begrudgingly exited and growled past the massive Desert Fire Resort on my right. This reminded me that I hadn't received the golf certificate from their resort yesterday as promised. I made a mental note to call them to complain as soon as I could, but first I drove past the entrance to my condo and up Mo's short driveway.

I wanted to give her the pick of my cosmetics to sample for a few days. It was always more challenging to return personal items that were slightly used, and I never wore that much make up anyway.

Mo greeted me at the door.

"I swear, just the sound of that thing makes my hormones do a little dance. I keep thinking some sexy hunk is going to emerge, rather than just you."

"Thanks, Mo, nice to see you too."

"Oh, you know I'm only teasing. I don't have eyes for anyone but Kane anyway." She automatically fluttered her eyelashes at me.

In spite of being married, Mo was pretty good at flirting. In school it had always amazed me how she could get whatever she wanted out of a man, professors included, all by the way she looked at them and spoke in that sugary tone that would sound ridiculous coming out of anyone else. She could never do my job; she'd always get her way and there'd never be any challenge.

"I brought you a little treat," I said, holding up the glossy red shopping bag.

"I knew there was a reason I loved you!" She smiled sweetly and wrapped her arms around me to give me a hug. She always gave me — and everyone else, for that matter — a hug if more than a day elapsed since

25

last seeing her. I didn't come from such a huggy family, but liked it from Mo just the same.

We walked into her cool, tiled foyer, and Mo immediately took the bag to her white leather couch and started unwrapping tissue paper.

"Mind if I use your phone?" I asked. I had my BlackBerry, but since it was a company device I didn't want to risk "Affluence, Inc." popping up on the caller I.D.

"Go right ahead . . . Oh! Bronzing Shimmer Powder — I love this stuff!"

I laughed. It didn't matter that Mo's skin color was paler than my own olive tone. She'd find a way to make it work. I strolled into the kitchen and clicked on my Black-Berry to search for Desert Fire's direct number. The phone rang twice before a pleasant male voice answered.

"Welcome to Desert Fire. My name is Tad. How can I help you today?"

"Hello, Tad. My name is Ren Edwards. I recently ordered a golf certificate online for my husband, for our anniversary. I paid extra to have it express delivered, but I haven't received it yet." I tried to give him a good sprinkling of information, but not too many of the details. That's part of the approach to see how good they are at listening

26

and probing.

"I'm sorry about that!" He sounded truly empathetic. "You bought a golf certificate through our shop? Let me look into that for you."

"Actually, I bought a certificate for your golf course *online*," I repeated.

"You bought that online?" he asked, sounding a little confused.

"Yes, from the Desert Fire Web site."

"Hmm." He paused, apparently to think.

Not a good sign.

"I don't think I can help you if you didn't buy it directly through us," he finally said.

"I did buy it *directly* through your resort Web site. It's not like I went through a third party."

"I'm sorry but we don't handle those . . . If you'd have come down to the shop, then I could've tracked that."

"Who do I need to speak with to resolve this?" I asked, getting a little peeved.

"I'm not sure . . ."

I audibly sighed.

"But I can look into it and call you back," he offered.

"Tad, this is my gift to my husband for our fifth wedding anniversary. It's tonight. That's why I specifically paid the fee to have you all overnight it to me. Now I don't have a gift for my husband." I managed to eke out an emotional crack in my voice.

Now Tad sounded alarmed.

"Mrs. Edwards, let me look into this for you right now, and I'll call you back within the hour. If I can't find out anything for you, I can give your husband fifty percent off one round of golf anytime — all he has to do is call and ask for me. That's a seventy-five-dollar discount on our green fees right now."

"My certificate was for five hundred dollars."

"Oh. Well, let me find out what's going on."

"I made the purchase on Monday around noon," I volunteered. He'd never get very far without at least the basics.

"Okay, Mrs. Edwards. I'm on it. I'll call you right back."

"Thanks," I said, wondering if he'd ask for my phone number.

"Have a great day, ma'am," he said and waited for me to say good-bye before disconnecting.

"This should be interesting," I said to Mo, who was now in her powder room dabbing anti-aging serum under her eyes.

"What is?" she asked, somewhat preoccupied.

"Looks like I may not have a gift to give my hubby on our special day."

"Oh well, honey, you're practically still in the honeymoon stage. I guarantee you that he'll be plenty distracted by your lingerie."

I laughed in agreement. She would be right, if there really *was* any man in my life. It was somewhat depressing to admit that I hadn't had the best of luck in that area. Sure, I'd met plenty of nice men, but the few I thought I'd clicked with had turned out to be married, or cheaters, or both. I was pretty cautious these days. In reality, I stuck to boxers and tees for sleeping. I had no doubt the lingerie would stay unwrinkled in its tissue paper until I returned it.

"I've got to go. I've got a mani-pedi at three — big night tonight."

"Thanks for the goodies, Ren. I'll bring 'em back over on Friday as usual."

Mo thoroughly enjoyed my perks, but always promptly returned whatever she'd borrowed on Friday mornings on her way to her yoga class. That's when I usually made my runs for returns. She knows how much my job means to me and would never jeopardize it.

"See you, Mo." I let myself out and slid behind the wheel of the Audi, allowing my spirits to lift a little. Even in a-hundred-plus-degree sunshine, it only felt slightly warm inside the car. I didn't burn my fingers on the seatbelt clip or steering wheel as I had in the white Volvo. Ah, the beauty of maximum ceramic window tint.

When I got home I could hear my phone ringing from outside my door. I let myself in and quickly lifted the receiver. It was Mo.

"Honey, some sweet thing from that golf course called and wanted to talk with you. They must have used the caller I.D. from your last call and traced it to me. Do you need the number to call him back?"

"No, I've got it. Tad, right?"

"That was it."

"I'll give him a call, thanks."

I didn't bother to replace the receiver, just clicked the phone off and right back on. I dialed the number that I still remembered from a few minutes earlier.

"Welcome to Desert Fire. My name is Tad. How can I help you today?"

"Tad, Mrs. Edwards here," I said, maybe a bit too snippily.

"Mrs. Edwards, thank you so much for calling me back. I asked around about the certificates, and it seems we do handle those in shop, after all. That form on the Web site is just a template that sends the info to us. How about that?"

"How about that," I repeated flatly.

"So, I can tell you now with confidence that we never got your order. I'm sorry, but I can take it again for you now, and you could come down to pick it up. And, like I said, I'll give your husband a seventy-five-dollar credit too. He can use that for golf, or in the shop, or even for lessons."

"Tad," I said, "for all you know, I could live in Flagstaff. Do you really think that inconveniencing me to come down to the resort to pick up that certificate on my anniversary, when I should be getting ready for a romantic dinner, is the best option for me?"

"You live in Flagstaff?" he asked, incredulous.

"No, Tad. I think you miss my point." I was now using my icy-customer-soon-to-be-lost-forever voice.

"Ma'am?"

"Tad?" Then I said the words. The ones that have come out of my mouth on so many prior occasions when the good people on the front line are either just not creative enough or not empowered enough to make it right for me: "May I speak to your manager please?"

Tad paused, apparently wounded that I didn't think he was handling the situation correctly, but he meekly agreed. Of course, the manager wasn't there at that precise moment, so he'd have to call me back. I sighed again, gave him my home number, and said I would be waiting.

After I hung up with Tad, I flipped open the laptop and made the expected entries. Then, knowing that I would be splurging on the experience of a four-star restaurant the following night, I found a Granny Smith apple and a yogurt in the fridge for dinner. I was just finishing the apple when the phone rang again. I glanced at the clock. If it was after 6:30 P.M., I didn't want to answer the phone — I was supposed to be on my way to a romantic dinner. It was only 5:00 P.M.

"Hello?" I answered, trying to sound inconvenienced.

"Mrs. Edwards?" a beautiful, smooth, but not-too-deep voice said to me.

"Yes?" I said, caught a little off guard by the sheer sexiness of the sound of those two words coming from that voice.

"My name is Adan Bennett. I'm the manager of Desert Fire Golf Course. Do you have a moment to speak with me about the gift certificate you ordered, or would you prefer that I call back at a different time? I understand that it's your anniversary."

My head was actually swimming a little, his voice was that mesmerizing. I shook my head once to clear it, then cleared my throat.

"No, thank you for calling Adam — I can speak with you now," I said, intentionally mispronouncing the name that he'd given me. He graciously did not correct me.

"Mrs. Edwards, I understand that you purchased a five-hundred-dollar golf certificate as an anniversary gift to give to your husband. First, please allow me to say how sincerely sorry I am that we disappointed you. I'd like to explain what happened, not to excuse us, but because I think we owe you that. Is that okay with you?" He paused, waiting for my reply. He didn't interrupt even when it was a few seconds before I responded. I was having trouble following his exact words, so enthralled was I with his voice.

"Yes, please . . ." I finally managed. This was ridiculous. I was going to have to pull myself together to do my job properly.

I listened, focusing on the words and not the tone, as he explained the mix-up that had occurred between my order and one other that had come in for the same amount, at the same time. The other order had ended up getting rushed while mine, in error, was following their usual processing time.

"I realize that this is not excusable, but again I offer my apologies."

Hmm. Sincere but not obsequious.

"May I be so bold as to ask you what you had intended the certificate to be used for?"

That *was* a little bold, but I decided to see whether or not he had a good reason for asking me.

"Well, I often visit the spa at your resort, and I always enjoy it so much that I thought it might be nice for my husband to experience your resort in his own way. I specifically purchased the certificate for enough money so that he and a buddy could go together," I explained.

"I see. Thank you. Mrs. Edwards," the captivating voice purred. "If it would be acceptable to you, I'd like to offer your husband a complimentary three rounds of golf during any time of the year."

"Oh, um, yes. I think that would be very nice of you. Thank you."

"And, Mrs. Edwards, do you think that your husband would prefer to have those three rounds on separate certificates to be used at different times, or on one certificate, instead?"

"Uh, I think one would be okay." I bit my

lower lip, trying to concentrate on remembering the details of the call and not this man's beguiling voice.

"Very well. Can I have one of our couriers bring the certificate to you tonight?"

I glanced around my very single-looking condo in a quick panic.

"Oh, no, that's not necessary. We're leaving soon for dinner so I'll just tell him about the gift."

"Very well. Please be assured that I will have the certificate sent by overnight mail to you tomorrow. I have the address from your original order."

"Great. Thank you, Adan," I said, wondering if it were possible or even wise to try to prolong the conversation just to keep him talking.

"Mrs. Edwards, because of the inconvenience you've experienced, I also want to offer you two complimentary spa treatments at our Desert Fire Day Spa for you and a friend."

"Oh?" I said, not bothering anymore to mask the surprise in my tone.

"I will ensure that a credit is set up in your name at the reception desk. You can use it anytime this year."

"Don't worry, I wouldn't let that credit get stale. I love your spa!" I almost gushed, allowing delight to creep in.

I could practically hear him smiling on the other end of the line.

"I'm pleased to hear that. If you have any further concerns, you can call me directly. It's Adan Bennett." He repeated his name, once more, for my benefit and gave me his direct extension.

"Thank you," I said.

"Have a good evening, Mrs. Edwards."

I reluctantly clicked the End button on my handset and let out a deep breath. I stared at the headset for a full minute. Wow. Nice recovery, yes, but *that voice.* That voice should be illegal! I set the phone down to make my notes in the spreadsheet and tried not to let the allure of his voice sway my objectivity. Or should I? Wasn't tone part of communication style? I made a few minor edits to what I had entered and snapped the lid shut. Another sigh.

"Happy anniversary," I said to no one. I went to the couch to spend the evening with my favorite two men, Ben and Jerry. I had to chuckle when I saw the name of the only flavor I had left in the freezer: "Chubby Hubby."

CHAPTER THREE

SPA DAY

Mo and I didn't waste any time booking our spa day. I called my boss to let him know why I was taking the day off on such short notice, and he told me to go ahead and chalk it up to "experience." That meant I could consider it a work day. Best job ever, I tell you.

Mo was already outside in the Volvo, honking her horn to hurry me. I grimaced and stuffed a bathing suit and light sweatpants into a duffle bag. It was still only 8:00 A.M. Everyone knows you don't honk in Scottsdale until after eleven unless you want some seriously cranky "clubbers" on your case. I jumped out into the entryway and pulled the door closed behind me, then waved to Mo, hoping to stymie another outburst.

"Wow, honey," she said when she saw me. "Just because we're going to the spa doesn't mean you can't try to be a little present-able."

I gave Mo the once-over. She was wearing full makeup, including foundation and powder, and her hair was sprayed into a respectably high pouf. She was wearing white yoga pants that hugged her thighs and a bright, lime green tank top.

"Wow, yourself," I commented. "I think you're supposed to wear more subtle colors for yoga."

"Green is a very soothing color," she said and revved out of the parking lot.

"I'm not sure neon qualifies," I teased her.

She gave me a huge smile and tilted her head to one side so that she could glare at me good-naturedly from under her dark eyelashes. Somehow she made it look flirtatious.

"You're going to have to teach me how to do that someday," I said as I twisted my light brown, shoulder-length hair up into a clip.

"Well, a little mascara wouldn't kill you, to start," said Mo.

"We're going to the spa. Two minutes in the steam room and you're going to look like something from a horror movie," I challenged. "Besides, it's not like we're going to be seeing any men there."

Desert Fire Day Spa had special rooms for couples' massages and a tiny, shared outdoor café for lunch, but otherwise the women and men had completely separate amenities. Thank goodness. Who wanted to worry about *that* during a day of relaxation? I'd never even had the nerve to book a male therapist.

Ten minutes later we were standing in a tastefully decorated lobby. The place oozed tranquility. Desert plants and cacti thrived in pots placed artfully against the bare walls. The floor was cool beige, tumbled tile. A large fountain tiled in complementary sage green lined a circular fountain in the middle of the room. A gentle river of rocks and trickling water circled the perimeter of the fountain. The sun shined through glass panes in the ceiling but managed not to feel too warm on our shoulders, and the entire room smelled vaguely of lavender and sage. I could practically feel the pupils in my eyes dilate in spite of the bright sunlight.

"Aaah," Mo sighed.

My sentiments exactly. There was almost no place I loved better than the spa, and Arizona really knew how to do the spa well, especially at the finer resorts. I stepped up to the desk and whispered my name to the woman in the sage green polo and beige shorts behind the counter.

"Good morning. I have reservations under the name Edwards."

The woman smiled serenely and tapped out my name soundlessly on her keyboard.

"Mrs. Edwards, here you are . . . and Mrs. Stemple with you?"

I nodded, not wanting to break the sound of the musical little river behind me.

"I see that you've spent time with us before. Welcome back," she said. "Your treatments today are complimentary, but would you like to leave a credit card number with us for lunch or any other incidentals you may wish to charge to your account?"

I nodded and handed her my personal gold charge card. I was already on work time and didn't feel like I should push the perks. She updated my account and handed back the card, smiling the same serene smile. I wondered if that was a qualification for the job.

"You'll each be enjoying the eighty-minute Desert Hot Stone Massage at ten and the Arizona Honey Facial at two. Would you like to make a reservation on the patio for lunch between treatments?"

"Please," I said, remembering a mouthwatering chipotle chicken salad croissant I had splurged on last time.

"You're all set, then. Hannah will take you back to the dressing rooms. Please enjoy your day."

She handed me a flyer with the group exercise schedule before I walked away. I flashed another grimace at Mo. "Do we really have to exercise on spa day? This is supposed to be like vacation."

"You'll relax better after we do," she assured me, trotting after Hannah, a large blond woman with a twisted braid.

I tried to concentrate on breathing instead of burning a hole into the seat of Mo's pants with my angry glare.

Breathe in. "Ohm." And breathe out. Breathe in again. "Ohm."

The sweaty palms of my hands slipped another inch forward on my yoga mat while beads of sweat trickled up my hairline, then down my nose, and landed in a tiny pool between my hands. Downward facing dog — what kind of cruel torture was that? I thought yoga was supposed to be relaxing.

I saw Mo dip her head closer to the mat and smile at me innocently from between her legs. I gritted my teeth and tried to remember why I hadn't just taken all four treatments for myself.

"And up . . . And breathe . . . And slowly

to the mat . . . Corpse pose now . . . ," the size-two pretzel at the front of the room ordered in that annoying, silky voice.

Corpse pose, at least that was more my pace. I lay still on my back with my palms facing up, willing my arms to feel less Jell-O-y.

"Namaste," I finally heard her say.

I forced myself off my sticky mat and noticed that the rest of the class had already transitioned to a seated position and were holding their hands together and bowing their heads. I gave a halfhearted nod and pulled my mat off the floor with another glare at Mo.

"Happy?" I almost snarled, but stopped. She did actually look happy . . . peaceful. Figured. Mo stayed behind for a minute to talk to the pixie-like instructor and I moped off to the showers.

The minute I entered the bathroom I felt my spirits lifting again. The scent of mango and mint wafted from the shower area. I pulled off my sweaty workout clothes and slipped under a large towel. I didn't want to get the soft, fluffy bathrobe we would wear for the rest of the day all sweaty, but I wasn't an exhibitionist either. I left the robe on the hook and headed into the first empty shower stall. Ten steamy minutes later, I emerged feeling renewed. I wrapped my hair in a smaller towel and headed back for my robe, then went upstairs to where the treatments were administered.

When I finally reached the dimly lit waiting area, Mo was already there reading a Southwestern gourmet-cooking magazine.

"I swear they do more with tomatoes, hot peppers and onions in this state than they do in Italy."

"Yeah, but it turns out a lot spicier," I pointed out.

"That's what I'm talking about. The spicier the better," she said, eyes twinkling.

I had a feeling we weren't talking about food anymore, but with Mo, I couldn't be sure. "I guess I wouldn't know," I said, sighing again. "Can we please talk about something else?"

"Sorry, honey, there's no *Car and Driver* in this pile." She waved her hand over the stack of glossy magazines spread in a perfect fan across the table.

"Very funny," I said, lying back on the squishy chaise and closing my eyes.

"I can't believe you people keep a fire going in the dead of summer," I heard Mo's slightly disapproving voice say.

I peeked an eye open to look at the gentle flames licking an artificial stack of logs in the gas fire pit near the center of the room.

"Uh-huh," I said, closing the eye. I was already feeling more relaxed.

"I'm sorry about the yoga," I heard Mo say. "I should have picked something a bit more your speed — like beginner stretching."

"I'm sorry I couldn't keep up," I murmured, allowing the toasty room and the soothing notes of guitar and Celtic harp to work their uncoiling effect on my muscles. I filled my lungs with eucalyptus-scented air, held it a count, then let it out slowly through my nose. I felt the tension ebb away and dissolve into the warm space around me.

"I'm sorry you're sorry," Mo said. "I should know by now that your idea of exercise is walking a few steps up the mall escalator."

"Well, I'm sorry . . ." I struggled to say something I'm sure would have been a snappy comeback, but drifted off before the words could form.

"I'm sorry," I heard a silky smooth voice say. It was deep and sexy, like the low growl of my engine. "I really am sorry about what happened, Mrs. Edwards. Can you let me make it up to you?"

A tall, faceless man wearing white jeans and a white T-shirt stretched tight across his muscular chest appeared out of the warm haze, rubbing his hands together as if to warm them up . . . or as if in anticipation of what was to come. He sat at the edge of the chaise, causing me to lean into his warm body. I shifted shyly away from him. He slowly lifted his hands and dropped the back of my robe. I peeked over my shoulder and saw that two bright red chili peppers had appeared in his hands.

"I thought this was a hot stone massage," I said, my voice weak with fascination.

"Hot *pepper* massage Mrs. Edwards," he whispered into my ear. "It's much better."

He began rubbing sensual circles over my shoulder blades with the peppers. "You see what I mean, Mrs. Edwards? Much better than hot stones, don't you think? Mrs. Edwards?" The voice purred deep in my ear. His tongue curled slightly around the 'r' sound in my name.

"Mrs. Edwards . . . Mrs. Edwards? . . . *Mrs. Edwards.*" A small but firm hand shook my arm, gently bringing me back to the surface.

"Huh?" I said, looking at the unfamiliar room. It took me a few seconds to remember where I was.

"Honey, you don't want to sleep the day away. You're going to miss all the good

45

stuff," Mo said, standing to greet her massage technician.

"You have no idea," I mumbled under my breath.

The woman still holding my sleeve smiled at me brightly.

"Mrs. Edwards? Are you ready for your massage now?"

Mo was waiting for me after my massage. I ambled somewhat drunkenly out of the dim corridor toward the waiting area, sipping cool lemon-water from a plastic cup.

"Now *that's* what I'm talking about," I gushed to Mo.

She looks energized by the massage, not weak-kneed like I felt, and she's glowing.

"You want to sit down for a minute?" She eyed me warily.

"Nope. I'm great," I said in a dreamy voice.

"Okay then . . ." She glanced nervously at the narrow staircase and back at me. "Lunch?"

"Anything you say."

The sense of euphoria clung to me as I sat poolside under the tall palms at a little round table on the patio with Mo. I lazily watched her swirl a sprig of mint around her Mojito.

"Are you sure that's such a good idea?" I asked with just the teensiest bit of concern. "You still have another treatment coming. I think you're supposed to be drinking a lot of water, not a lot of rum."

"Water-smater. What? Do we live in a desert?" Mo said.

I raised my eyebrow at her.

"Hot waiter at two o'clock," she said.

I followed her gaze. When Mo's right, she's right. This was more than just a hot waiter. This was a smoldering desert god. Every female head turned his way as he strode toward us, clad in beige shorts and a navy polo that hugged his lean muscles. He was very tall, at least six-three, and older than the other waiters — in his early thirties probably, with short, dark hair mussed up in a good way, and beautiful milk-caramel-colored skin. He looked so commanding walking toward us that I had to suppress the urge to fly to my knees and bow. When he reached our table, I was startled to see that his eyes weren't brown, as I had expected; they sparkled bluer than the pristine pool water. He smiled a crooked, mischievous smile, revealing perfect white teeth. The sexy masseur from my dreams had nothing on this guy. Seeing us relax there seemed to bring him great pleasure.

"Mrs. Edwards?" he asked smoothly.

Oh boy.

Mo kicked me under the table.

"Yes," I squeaked.

"Mrs. Edwards," he repeated, holding out his strong, tan hand.

It was *his* voice. I felt a twinge of panic for no real reason that I could think of. I straightened in my chair.

"I'm Adan Bennett. We spoke on the phone the other day," he kindly reminded me.

"Of course," I managed to say, holding out my hand weakly. He grasped it, gently wrapping his long fingers around mine, and shook my hand as if there was actually a live human on the other end instead of a limp fish. I felt a little hum of electricity in my head when his palm made contact, very warm and slightly rough. I noticed he wasn't wearing a ring and his fingers were evenly tanned.

"I don't mean to interrupt your luncheon, but I saw in the computer that you had made your spa reservations, and I didn't want to miss this opportunity to introduce myself and see if there was anything that you needed."

"Anything that I . . . needed?" I repeated

more to myself than to him.

Adan nodded and smiled, looking from me to Mo. I chanced a glance at Mo to catch her reaction — wondering if this stunning man was having this effect on both of us, or just on me. Mo had a giddy smile plastered on her face and hadn't taken her eyes off Adan. She absently lifted her drink to her mouth. Her straw, instead of reaching her lips, plunged partially into one of her nostrils. My eyes widened. She giggled and quickly pulled down the glass, but the straw stayed where it was, sticking out of her nose. Horrified, I reached forward and snatched it, then buried my hand and the straw in the folds of my robe.

My robe! How embarrassing! I was sitting here talking to this striking man while wearing a bathrobe. Well, technically, I wasn't talking. Maybe I should be talking.

Adan was politely keeping his eyes off Mo now, and looking directly at me. It felt like he was scrutinizing every line of my face. A look crossed his face that caused his forehead to crinkle for a flash, but it disappeared when he spoke again.

"I can see that you are enjoying yourselves, so I won't interrupt you further. Please don't hesitate to call if you need anything." He reached into his pocket and placed a business card flat on the table, then smiled again and turned to walk away. It would take every ounce of control not to sneak a peek at what I knew would be his perfectly formed backside, and being that I was already in a semi-relaxed state and had just been taken off guard, I gave up the effort. *Oh yes.* Perfectly formed.

"Excuse me," I heard Mo trying to tap through my distracted gaze. "Who is Adan Bennett?" she demanded.

"No one," I said as a terrible realization hit me.

"Not buying it. He was someone, and by the way he was looking at you, I'd say he thought *you* were someone too."

"What?"

"Are you going to sit there and tell me you didn't notice him practically drooling over you? It looked like he was trying to keep from pouncing, and finally had to give up and leave."

"What?" I asked incredulously.

"Come on, Ren. Who is this guy, and why haven't you mentioned him before?"

I picked up his business card with my fingers and gently traced the edge. *Adan Bennett, Manager — Desert Fire, Golf Pro Shop Services.*

"Adan Bennett," I finally say flatly. "He

manages the golf program here at the resort."

"You make it sound like you don't like him." Mo squinted at me, trying to read through my dazed exterior.

"Oh, I think I like him."

"Then what's the problem? Is he married or something?"

"No," I said frowning. "But *I* am."

CHAPTER FOUR
SHOPPING SPREE

"Why don't you just tell him the truth?" Mo asked, clearly not understanding how deeply my charade had gone.

"I can't. I'd be humiliated," I said.

"Okay, so then you just left your rotten husband — it happens all the time," Mo assured me.

"After just celebrating five blissful years of marriage a week ago?"

"Sure. You caught the creep with the nanny and that pushed you over the edge."

"I don't have any kids — remember?" I said, exasperated. "And I don't want to come off as some rebounding basket case. Honestly, would you go out with someone who just left their spouse a week ago?"

"Sweetie, you forget how happily married I am. I wouldn't leave Kane for all the golf courses in Scottsdale. He's the sweetest, most selfless man. Why, just last night . . ."

"Enough, please!"

"Okay, I can see that you're a little edgy here."

"Wait a minute, golf courses in Scottsdale," I said.

"That's what I just said," Mo said.

"No, golf, that's it! I can book golf lessons for myself. That way, I could get close to him — find out if I'm really attracted to him or if I was just taken off guard by his manner. It's not worth blowing my cover if he's not everything I think he *might* be." I thought back to the soothing voice, the calm demeanor, the deep blue eyes. "I don't even know him, after all."

"Yeah, that'll work. Snuggle up into the big old arms of the golf pro while he teaches you how to grip the club, so you can objectively decide if he's really your soul mate or just some hunk you're lusting after. No danger there."

"Do you have a better idea?" I asked, daring her to speak it.

"The truth?" She spoke it. Mo never was intimidated by a dare.

"Definitely no. I won't humiliate a perfect stranger for no good reason."

"Ah, but if you had a reason . . ."

"Stop it. You're taking golf lessons with me and that's that."

Mo rolled her eyes, but I knew she would

53

be game. Working on her tan all day was way too boring and she wasn't about to get a job with all the fun she had vicariously through mine.

"Kane's been trying to squeeze in an awful lot of games before those green fees go up," she said tentatively. "I swear he goes golfing at least three times a week with two of his buddies from work. It's getting expensive," she admitted. "Think our lessons will qualify as an 'experience'?"

"Oh don't worry," I said. "I have absolutely no doubt that they'll qualify as an experience."

Before I could start taking golf lessons from the potential man of my dreams, I had to make sure I was outfitted with the right equipment. That meant a trip to Nordstrom's, of course. I wasn't worried about golf clubs or bags. That equipment would be included for now, and I'd already purchased our group lessons, using my personal charge for Mo's and letting Affluence Index pick up mine. I was very careful to sketch out a good strategy for what I was looking for and how it would be measured, from a customer-experience-assessor standpoint, of course. Now I had only to shop.

Mo apparently had some domestic errands to run, so I was meeting her at the outdoor shopping plaza before lunch. We planned to hit the racks first, then try the nearby high-end seafood restaurant that I'd heard so much about. You wouldn't expect seafood to be any good in Arizona, but you'd be amazed at the quality at some of the finer establishments. This place specialized in clams. Thinking back to how Adan had looked when he first approached our table, so confident and pleased to see us . . . I was glad they didn't specialize in oysters. I didn't need any more encouragement.

When I reached the athletic department Mo was already trying on a cropped white hoodie that bared her entire midsection. Her lower half was squeezed into a tight, very short, black Nike skirt with white stripes racing down the sides.

"Um, we're going to be golfing, remember?" I said.

Mo did a little dance as she spun in a circle in front of the dressing room mirror. "But this is so cute," she said.

"Cute, yes, appropriate, no." I looked at the tag that was dangling from her wrist. "This is a tennis outfit anyway, and Mo, did you even look at the price tag? I'm pretty sure your car payment isn't this high."

Mo frowned and slipped the top up over

her head. "You really know how to spoil a party sometimes," she said.

"Correction — I *am* the party. I'm buying, remember?" I patted my shoulder bag where my company's charge card was safely tucked. "Is there a salesperson anywhere to help us?"

"Ugh," Mo said. "I can't stand salespeople haunting me while I try to shop. I already sent her away."

"Okay, Mo, but that's part of the experience. Did you see which way she went?"

I needn't have asked. A moment later, a pretty blond, who had a sleek ponytail and was dressed in a tastefully expensive beige skirt and white blouse, appeared behind me as if she had a special radar that told her just exactly when she was needed. I glanced around the dressing room quickly, looking for electronic bugs.

"Good morning. Is there anything I can help you with?" she asked me sweetly, but a little haughtily, I thought. *Treat me poorly at your peril, lady.*

"Yes, thanks. We're trying to find some appropriate outfits for golf. We'll need at least three each, maybe more." It didn't look good for my status as a wealthy American to be seen in repeating outfits.

"I see. Well, we don't have golf apparel

specifically, but any of our outdoor leisure apparel would be suitable." She eyed Mo standing there in her bra and tight black skirt. Mo eyed her back.

"Of course, if you can give me a sense of your . . . *style,* I can make some recommendations," she said.

"Gwen Stefani. Anne Hathaway." I pointed first to Mo, then to myself. "But please, maybe a post-baby, slightly more *modest* Gwen?" I suggested. I didn't want Mo grabbing all the attention; after all, she already had the man of her dreams.

"I understand," the woman said.

In no time at all, we were both perspiring lightly from the effort of trying on so many different combinations. I slipped into a white, sleeveless tennis dress and stepped out into better light to view how I looked. I smiled appreciatively. This one was all right. Mo stepped out just after me in a loose, white polo and long, plaid Bermuda shorts.

"I look like Kane's boss, and he's a man," she said with a pout. "I think."

"Okay, I won't make you buy that. But not too much skin — there must be something here that you think is acceptable."

She finally settled on several classic white skorts, and a few more femininely cut polos, two of which dipped so low I wondered if she'd end up with some painful sunburn. I was happy with two other dresses similar to the first, a few fitted polos in soft colors, and two matching, lightweight visors. After that, we hit the local sporting-goods store for special golf shoes and socks. When we finally sat down to a late lunch we were nearly exhausted.

"I had no idea golf could be so tiring," Mo commented, not looking up from her menu, "and I'm so parched!" She ordered a Cosmo.

I softly snorted.

After placing our order with an annoyingly pretentious waiter (I made some scathing notes in my BlackBerry), I reviewed our plans with Mo. "So, we'll be taking lessons on Mondays, Wednesdays and Fridays at nine A.M., for two and a half hours a day. That still works for you, right?"

"Oh sure," Mo said. "In fact, that's usually when Kane golfs with his buddies too. They put in so many late hours and weekends that he likes to be flexible and let them come in late. It'll be nice to see him for a little in the morning for once."

"Really? He golfs three times a week now?" I quickly calculated how much that was in green fees. I wondered how they got by so well without Mo working. "You know, you can have the gift certificate I got as compensation. It's for three rounds. I'll probably never use them myself, and it's not something I can return," I suggested.

"He'll love that — thanks! But, you know, he just got another promotion at work. He's overseeing about a hundred and fifty people now."

"Mo, that's great!" I said, genuinely pleased for them.

"Golf is his way of blowing off steam . . . if you know what I mean."

I always knew what she meant. I just wished she didn't bring up the gory details three times a day. It was like eating a cheeseburger in front of a homeless person. Geez. They'd been married three years now. When did the honeymoon end?

"Uh-huh," I said, stuffing a mini-crab cake into my mouth.

"You know, did I tell you, the other night —" She started to giggle.

"Say, Mo?" I said quickly, swallowing the lump of crab to change the subject. "Who does Kane usually go golfing with?"

"Just some guys from work, but their wives apparently aren't as gracious about it as I am." She looked pleased with herself. "Though I suppose their husbands might not being doing quite as well financially as we are." She looked thoughtful for a moment, then shrugged it off. "You know, I remember when Kane was just starting out . . ."

I listened to her prattle on pleasantly about her early years with Kane after college. Her eyes lit up with animation at the memory. I smiled warmly at her and thought how nice it must be to have found someone who could make you truly happy, because I had no doubt that's exactly what both Kane and Mo were. And that was one reason I wasn't willing to settle for anything less.

CHAPTER FIVE

GROUP LESSONS

I was still lying on the cold bathroom tile floor when I heard Mo let herself in.

"What a *glorious* morning." I could hear her echoing through my hallway. "Did you know the temperature dropped overnight? I think it's only ninety-eight degrees out there. I may get to wear my Uggs again sooner than I thought. Ren?"

"In here," I groaned weakly.

"What happened to you?" Mo stood in the bathroom doorway, frowning down on me.

"Sick . . . clams . . . ," I said limply by way of explanation. Fortunately Mo and I have plenty of practice conveying our meaning to each other with few words.

"From lunch yesterday? I knew there was something fishy about eating seafood in Arizona. You should have stuck with the Angus burger like I did — or at the very least a Cosmo might have killed off whatever is bothering you."

If I had had enough strength to roll my eyes, I would have. As it was, I lay there flat on the floor.

"Sorry, honey, I didn't mean to rub it in. Do you feel any better now?"

I nodded pathetically. "Just . . . wiped out . . ."

"Okay then, let's get you cleaned up and into bed."

Luckily, Mo was not squeamish about the more-practical matters of life. She had no problem scraping me off the floor and wiping my face clean with a cool towel. Then she ran a shower for me and held me straight under the stream of water until I felt steady enough to continue without her. The hot water hitting me in the face inched me closer to consciousness. I finished washing my hair, then chose an inoffensive ginger-and-white-tea-scented gel from the collection of bottles crowding my shower rack and worked it into a sudsy lather across my skin. When I had finished with a cold rinse, I stepped out of the shower. I felt mostly human again.

Mo eyed me skeptically.

I ambled shakily to my closet and pulled out the white, sleeveless athletic dress.

"You're not seriously thinking of going

today?" Mo asked.

"Of course I am. I'm not going to miss the first lesson."

"I didn't think you cared about the actual lessons."

"I don't, but that doesn't mean I want to make it any harder for myself. I'm already likely to make a fool of myself, and I don't want to up the odds any."

Mo shook her head while she watched me struggle into the dress and tie my hair into a wet pony tail, then slip a visor over it. I had planned to blow-dry my hair, but knew I needed to save my strength for the lesson. I wobbled into the bathroom and dabbed some blush onto my cheeks, chin and forehead so I wouldn't look as ghostly white, and then I swiped some mascara on my lashes and poked myself in the eye while the applying the second coat. The eye immediately started running so hard that I had to hold a washcloth over it for several minutes. When I pulled my hand away Mo turned away from me and I could see her shoulders shaking in suppressed laughter. I looked in the mirror and understood why. One eye was bright pink and rimmed in so much smeared, black mascara that I resembled Captain Jack Sparrow. My face was now so pale that the blush I had applied looked like a bad rash. I groaned and drenched the washcloth in warm water and then started scrubbing my face. I decided not to try to start over. "Au naturel" was going to have to be good enough for today.

I brushed my teeth for the third time and covered my face and shoulders in sunscreen before joining Mo in the kitchen, where she'd gone to find something tame for me to eat. She was already holding a baggie of saltines when I entered the room.

"All better now?" she asked with just the trace of a snicker.

I grunted and grabbed the bag of saltines.

"Let's go. We're going to be late if you have to drive," I mumbled.

Most of the group that had signed up for lessons was already assembled in plastic, white chairs on the pristinely cut lawn outside the golf shop. The gathering in the front row consisted of two older ladies, probably in their late fifties, and a sweet-looking teenage girl, listening to tunes from her iPod and acting as if she'd rather be just about anywhere else. In the back row were two women in their early forties wearing cowboy hats, jean shorts, and thick leather belts adorned with enormous, metal cowboy belt buckles. Then it was me, Mo and . . . ugh, the perky little yoga instructor from the spa . . . What was *she* doing here?

I looked to Mo for moral support but she wasn't paying attention. She was waggling her fingers at Kane, who was huddled with two other men in his golf party nearby. They were just getting ready to tee off.

As soon as we were seated, Adan and a young blond man in white shorts and a navy polo exited from the golf shop and stood authoritatively in front of the group. My heart started palpitating a bit as I looked at Adan. He was more handsome than I remembered. He was about a half foot taller than the younger man, and though they were both unarguably good-looking, Adan had a presence that exuded masculinity — a presence the other man lacked. Adan looked over the group as if to appraise the people in it, and caught my eye. He seemed startled to see me, but the sentiment quickly passed and he smiled invitingly, nodding slightly to acknowledge me. Then, to my utter horror, he said something to the younger man, patted his back as if to impart confidence, then strode toward the clubhouse, which was located closer to the main section of the resort.

Adan had taken only a few steps when the yoga instructor bolted out of her chair and stopped him by looping her right arm around his left, pulling him back slightly. He looked down at her with obvious surprise. I could only see her profile, so I couldn't make out the words, but she chatted animatedly with him for a few minutes while he listened without expression. He finally said something brief to her and she smiled in appreciation, then practically skipped back, casting him a flirtatious glance over her shoulder just before she reached the group. This time, she took a seat in the front row. I silently rejoiced that he had already turned his back to her by then, so had missed the flirtatious look.

"Good morning class!" the enthusiastic blond bellowed at us. He flashed a white smile that looked too bright in his tanned face. I ignored him and wistfully watched Adan walk away, trying not to be too obvious. The teenager sat up a little straighter when the blond instructor started talking.

"Welcome to Beginner's Golf at Desert Fire. My name is Tad, and I'm going to be your instructor for the next three weeks. Since we're going to be spending so much time together, let's start with a brief introduction. What's your name, young lady?" He flashed a smile at one of the older ladies in the front row.

"I'm Flo," she said, chuckling softly at his flattery.

"And your younger sister here?" he asked, referring to the lady sitting next to her.

"Shirley." The woman giggled, shaking her head good-humoredly.

"Lovely. It's a pleasure to have you here, ladies. And of course some of you may already know Karen from our Wellness and Fitness program. She's a student here today just like the rest of you." He smiled at Karen, who actually twisted backward in her chair to give the rest of us a lively little wave.

"I may throw up again," I said to Mo under my breath.

"And next to Karen we have . . . ?" He paused to allow the teenage girl to fill in her name. She looked awed by Tad, and he had to repeat his question before she responded.

"Casey Carpenter," she finally managed.

"And in the back row . . . ?" Tad continued, looking at me.

"I'm Ren Edwards," I said with as much enthusiasm as I could muster, which was very little.

"Oh, Mrs. Edwards! It's me, *Tad,* from the other week on the phone — remember?" he said energetically. "I'm so glad we were able to get your little situation straightened out." He winked as if keeping an inside

67

secret. "I just met your husband this morning, in fact. We checked him in with the rest of his party for the three free rounds." He beamed at me, clearly satisfied with the display of generosity.

I looked sharply at Mo.

"Husband?" I hissed.

Mo shrugged and introduced herself to the group, eager to keep the ball moving and me from making a scene.

"Hi, I'm Mary Jo Stemple." She flashed her own sunny smile at the group and turned toward the two middle-aged women sitting to her left. We learned that their names were Brenda and Donna. Mo immediately started referring to them as "Butch and Sundance" behind their backs.

I was starting to feel a little nauseated again, and I wasn't sure if it was because the sun was picking up in strength as it crept higher in the sky, or if it was due to the disappointment I was feeling at finding out that Tad, not Adan, was going to be our instructor. I nibbled on another saltine as I tried to listen to Tad talk about Lesson One, Part A: Golf Safety and Etiquette.

I felt my eyes glaze over as Tad droned on. I tried to remember the exact expression that Adan had made when he'd noticed me in the group. Yes, he did smile, but before that there'd been something I couldn't place — maybe not so much like surprise, but more like . . . dread. Of course he would dread my being here. He probably thought I was after some more freebies, and he'd already been overly generous. I slid down further in my chair and wished I had stayed home in bed after all.

". . . And that," I heard Tad saying, "is something you never want to forget unless you want to tick off a whole bunch of other golfers." A little wave of laughter rumbled through the group while they nodded appreciatively.

I looked up questioningly at Mo, but she was listening intently to Tad's next topic, Part B: Golf Equipment.

Lovely. I tried to listen to Tad.

"So there are generally fourteen clubs in a set, consisting of drivers, woods, irons and a putter," he was saying while pulling clubs from a nylon bag. "Since most of a golfer's time is spent on the green, the putter is the most important club to feel comfortable with. A good putter that feels just right when you hold it in your hands is worth its weight in gold."

The teenager raised her hand tentatively. Tad looked amused when he called on her.

"Yes, Casey?"

"Sorry, but what's a green?"

"Excellent question, Casey," he said. "Please everyone, there's no dumb question except the question you don't ask. The green is the closely cropped area of grass directly surrounding each hole . . ."

Casey listened obediently, nodding.

"Most golf courses consist of eighteen holes, a front nine and a back nine . . ."

I couldn't listen to this much longer, though it seemed like Tad held the rest of the audience captive, I watched while, in the distance, Kane and his buddies purchased beverages from a cart girl. I wondered which one had masqueraded as Mr. Edwards. Darn. I wish I'd thought of that before giving Mo the certificate. The worst part was that Tad had used the word "we": "We checked him and his party in . . ." Did that mean that Adan also thought one of them was my husband?

I squinted at them in the distance. Kane was by far the best catch, though that purple Diamondbacks ball cap he was wearing was clearly a fashion faux pas. One of the others had a potbelly and looked to be balding under his golf cap. The other one wasn't wearing a cap and I could see he had a full head of hair at least. I suppose he could have been called handsome, but it looked

70

like he was sort of harassing the cart girl, leaning way too closely into her and looking like he might grope her at any second.

The lessons couldn't get over quickly enough for me. As we filed along the gravel path leading back toward the clubhouse, Adan exited the double glass doors with something red in his hand. Little Miss Om picked up her pace a bit and tried to edge toward the front of the group. Her face fell visibly when he walked right past her and stopped in front of me.

"Mrs. Edwards," he said, his voice practically caressing the words.

"Please, call me Ren." I begged.

"All right, Ren." He smiled down at me, blocking out the sun and enveloping me in his long, cool shadow. "Your husband left this behind in the club this morning." He held out a bright red Cardinals ball cap.

Great, it was the groper then.

"I was going to run it out to him myself, but I've got a planning meeting I need to be at and I really can't be late." He looked down at me apologetically. "Would you like to take it home for him, or should I leave it with Tad?"

"Um . . ." I eyed the ball cap. It looked like it had never been washed. A dark sweat line stained the inside perimeter. "I'll take it," I said with defeat.

"Thank you, Mrs. Ed . . . Ren," he said. "I'm sorry even to have asked but . . ." He ran his fingers through his black hair and didn't finish the sentence. His eyes looked conflicted for a moment, but again, before I could be certain, the look was gone. "Are you stopping in for a drink?" he asked, indicating the clubhouse.

I looked at Mo, who was nodding encouragingly.

"Not today," I said wistfully. My stomach was telling me I'd better get home soon.

At that moment, Karen, who had been practically straining herself to hear our conversation, popped up behind Adan.

"It's so hot. Who wants to join me for a drink?" she said, brightly, though it was obvious that she was directing her comment at Adan. Butch and Sundance didn't give her the time of day, and Casey had already shrugged off since Tad was no longer part of the party. The two older ladies claimed they were meeting their husbands for lunch.

Karen eyed Mo carefully.

"I drove her." Mo pointed at me.

"So, just you and me then?" Karen looked cheerfully up at Adan.

"Another time perhaps — I really need to get to that meeting," he said, but he looked at me when he spoke. Then he turned and headed for the main lobby, leaving me in a blaze of hot sun.

"Honey, do you need me to draw you a picture? When a man you like asks if you'll have a drink, you say 'I will if you will.' Actually, that works in a bunch of other scenarios too. You'd do well to remember it next time," Mo scolded me on the way back to the Volvo.

"I couldn't. Aside from the fact that I'm about to heave, he not only thinks I'm married, but now he's actually *met* my husband." I groaned.

"That's Andy's cap. He wears it all the time," Mo said, eyeing it with obvious disgust.

"I can tell." I held it out in front of me between my thumb and index finger as if it were a dead snake.

"I'll kick Kane for you when he gets home. Andy's not the kind of guy you want representing you out in the world. Frank would have been better. Andy is a . . . a . . ."

"Weasel?" I offer.

"Ferret," she countered.

I sighed. Maybe Adan hadn't noticed. What was I thinking? What difference did it make? Either way, he thinks that he's my husband. Ugh!

"Look, maybe this is a good thing," Mo said, interrupting my thoughts.

I looked at her like she was a stroke short of a birdie — or would that be a stroke more than a birdie?

"No, really. Think about it. What better way is there to get to know someone without any threat of a romantic relationship? You could actually try to befriend the guy and get to see what he's *really* like."

I thought about that for a second. Maybe she was right. Maybe this was a great opportunity, after all. Men and women could be friends, right? If I could get to know Adan better as a person, I might be able to get past the dizziness I felt every time I managed to meet his disarming eyes, and I could get to be my *real* self around him too. The real self that had been lying to him since the second we'd met, that is.

"Interesting concept," I said noncommittally.

"Think about it. I'll drop you off so you can get some sleep," Mo said, taking the cap from me between her own two fingers. "Call me when you're ready to talk. I have a few ideas."

Oh boy.

CHAPTER SIX
THE RUSE

I went over Mo's plan in my mind again as I pulled my Audi into an end parking spot under the shadowy canopy of a mesquite. She wanted me to pretend to be so hopeless at golf that I couldn't possibly keep up with the group. Then she would drop a hint to Tad that maybe I should look into private lessons. I thought she was being a bit optimistic to think he'd give up on me after only two lessons, but was willing to give it a shot.

We had already called the club anonymously the night before and found out that Adan was the only one who gave private lessons, and they weren't cheap. If everything went according to plan, it would be more than worth it.

"Don't forget the plan," Mo said, unnecessarily.

"Sadly, I am sure I will have to do very little acting today. You know how pathetic I am at sports."

"Golf's not like a real sport. Little old ladies can do it," she said.

"If it requires coordination, it's a sport," I argued.

"Text messaging requires coordination," she said.

"I rest my case." I never used a cell phone unless it was an emergency and I didn't even know how to text someone — keeping track of notes in the BlackBerry presented enough of a challenge.

"Just remember —"

"Got it," I said, shooting my eyes in the direction of the clubhouse we were passing. Adan and the yoga pixie were sitting at a table on the patio drinking orange juice from plastic bottles. Karen's face was positively radiant, but Adan was staring off at the mountains in the distance, looking distracted.

"Try not to glower. You don't look half bad today," Mo said.

I reminded myself that she was right. Sure, Karen was petite and perky, and had the figure of a lithe panther, but I had cleaned up pretty good today too. After turning in early the last two nights I had given myself plenty of time to primp and prepare this morning. I was even wearing mascara.

I leaned into Mo to direct her off the path and onto the patio, where I slid into one of the cast-iron chairs as gracefully as I could. I draped one of my freshly shaven legs over the other one and angled my body toward Adan and Karen while I leaned my upper body toward Mo as if deep in conversation.

There. Let Little Miss Five Foot Three compete with the fifteen sleek inches of my shin bone. My long legs had always been one of my best features.

A snort of laugher escaped from Mo's lips. The sound caught Adan's attention and he looked up at us. I peeked under the pretense of looking for a menu. He looked frustrated. I felt my stomach knot up and I turned away quickly. I was telling Mo that I'd changed my mind about a drink when I felt him standing behind me.

"Good morning," he said pleasantly. "The clubhouse isn't open this early, but there is complimentary juice and water in the reception area if you'd like it."

"Oh, um, no thanks. We just decided we should get going — don't want to be late for lessons," I said, loath to have him think that I wanted to take advantage of anything else complimentary.

Mo kicked me under the table.

I winced. She'd better not have bruised my perfect shin.

Adan seemed uncomfortable for a moment as he watched us. "Well, you ladies have a nice day. Be careful out there — you actually get to swing a club today." He started to walk away.

"Thanks," I said.

Mo kicked me again.

I clenched my teeth and gave her a death stare. She pursed her lips back at me.

"Um . . . excuse me," I said.

Adan stopped and turned back to face me. I couldn't help but think that he shouldn't be allowed to unleash those piercing blue eyes on unsuspecting women without a permit.

"Yes?"

"Well, we were just talking about stopping back in for a drink later on, and we thought it might be fun if you'd like to join us . . . to . . . um . . . maybe give us some pointers."

"Free pointers, huh?" he said in a teasing tone. "Thanks, but actually I have another commitment for this afternoon."

Ugh! I bit my lip. Why did I say that? I didn't want free pointers — I just wanted *him*. At least I thought I wanted him. I *definitely* wanted to get to know him.

Adan looked at me as if waging some battle in his head.

"But if you're free Friday after lessons, I'd be pleased to sit and talk with you then." He looked at me hesitantly, almost like he was hoping I would say no.

"Okay, sure," I said.

"Sorry, I can't," Mo gleefully apologized. "I've got an appointment, but don't let me stop the two of you."

Adan's face fell just slightly, and now he looked almost scared. What must he think of me!

"If you'd rather not —" I offered.

He seemed to be weighing his options. Politeness inevitably won out.

"Of course I'd still like to meet with you . . . I'll see you on Friday," he said resolutely.

Karen, still sitting at the table behind him, had closed her eyes and was breathing deeply as if trying to gain control over some base emotion. I smiled smugly to myself as I rose from the table and signaled to Mo to get moving.

"What was *that?*" I looked at Mo accusingly as she drove a little white golf ball two hundred yards across the field.

"Nice grip, Mary Jo! You're really getting

into the swing of things, if you'll pardon my pun." Tad beamed at Mo as he supervised our natural golf swings. I figured that was code for trying to figure out how bad we were before he gave us some real instruction.

Mo grinned at me. "Hey, if this works out I may actually be able to go golfing with Kane. That would be so much fun!"

"Pardon me for not sharing your enthusiasm. This stinks. I'm going to be the worst one here," I grumped.

"I thought that was the point, remember?" Mo prompted me.

"Sure, but you don't have to go and be all naturally athletic on me."

We looked at each other and burst out laughing. No one could ever realistically call Mo naturally athletic, unless you counted being able to stretch down and paint your toenails without bending your knees. I guessed golf wasn't like other sports, after all. I decided to try to be more supportive of her.

"Your turn," Mo said.

Tad had been pacing behind the group, which was lined up at the driving range, so that he could assess everyone's skill as they took a shot. Now he paused behind me and watched. I glanced nervously at Mo. She winked back.

"Here goes nothing," I said. I gripped my club as tightly as I could with my sweaty palms and raised my arms swiftly into the air behind me without bending my elbows. Wait, why weren't my elbows bending? I didn't have to think about it long. The next moment, I realized that my golf club was sliding out from between my palms and, in what seemed like slow motion, I watched it fly airborne toward Tad, who was standing right behind me. He ducked just in time and it clunked against the ground with a sickening ping.

Mo stared at me with huge eyes, as if even she was shocked that I could have made such a disastrous move.

"Oh! I'm so sorry, Tad! I don't know what . . . I really didn't mean to . . . It must have been the sunscreen left over on my hands or —"

Tad held up one hand in front of me to stem my stream of words. "No harm, no foul. Okay group, let's bring it back in." He motioned for the group to return their clubs and head back for some more theoretical work before anyone else was subjected to possible beheading.

I sheepishly hung my head and collected the untouched ball from my tee.

"Nice one," Mo said once she'd recovered.

"I was trying to whiff the ball, not catapult the club!" I hissed.

"Well, you're off to a great start, anyway. I wouldn't be surprised if our boy there was begging Adan to take you on after a full day of this."

The teenager passed us as we were talking and stifled a snicker. When I caught her eye, she smiled apologetically. The yoga instructor followed behind her and kept pace with us.

"Don't worry about it, Rin — your yin and yang are just misaligned."

"It's *Ren,*" I corrected, probably a little too sharply.

"Well, some creative visualization could do wonders for you. I have a class on Tuesdays if you're interested. You and Mary Jo could try the first class for free to see if you liked it, though it doesn't look like Mary Jo will really need it."

She smiled sweetly at Mo. Mo smiled back, but not too warmly. Mo knows where her loyalties lie.

"Thanks, but no thanks, Karen."

"Offer's still open if you change your mind," she said, then bounded ahead to join the others.

Tad spent the next hour harping on how

the golfer's grip was fundamental to the game and how a poor grip will cause the game, and potentially any bystanders, to suffer. He winked at me when he made the joke, but I pretended not to notice. Then he talked about the three grips we were going to try to learn: the interlocking grip, the baseball grip and something called the Vardon grip.

"That's the one they use on *Star Trek,* the Vardon grip," Mo whispered to me, giggling at her own joke. I rewarded her with a chuckle of my own; after all, she'd more or less stood beside me during Karen's little pity-assault.

We spent the last hour back on the field, practicing our grips with our "natural swings" but without trying to hit any balls. I managed not to almost-decapitate anyone else, but I did jam my club into the grass so many times that my arms felt a permanent vibration from my wrists to my elbows.

Tad tried to give me some pointers to keep me from hacking any bigger of a hole into the tender ground in front of me, but I managed to overcorrect anything he suggested. I caught him shaking his head to himself behind my back, and after that he tried to spend more of his time with Casey and the others, who were clearly more promising pupils. I saw Mo slip over to him during one of my particularly violent attacks on the grass, and she whispered something in his ear. He glanced at me furtively and nodded.

By the end of the lesson he had already managed to corner me, telling me about how his sister was a terrible golfer until she took private lessons, and that now she was a scratch player.

"A scratch player?" I asked.

"Yeah. Oh, I forget you newbies don't know all the terms. A scratch player is someone who can basically hold her own on the course. She's up to par."

"Do you think I could ever be a scratcher?" I asked with innocent eyes, deciding to play up the moment.

"Uh, it's not a scratcher — that's a lottery ticket — but a scratch player, and sure, maybe you could get there with a lot of practice and the right instruction."

"The right instruction?" I prompted artfully.

"Well, yeah. But you might need a little more specialized instruction — more than what you can get with the group, something with a little more individual attention." He was starting to look nervous.

"Individual attention? Like from you?" I said, starting to feel just a little sorry for him, but not sorry enough to stop the charade.

"From me? Well, yeah, sure, I can try to pay as much attention to you as I can while you're in the group, but there are the others too — and two and a half hours goes by pretty fast divided by eight players."

I didn't say anything. I was going to make him paint me a picture.

"So what I'm saying is that you might want to consider taking *private* lessons."

"Private lessons?" I feigned ignorance. "Do you offer private lessons here?"

"Oh yeah, sure. We offer them when there's a need and an interest. Adan teaches them. I could have him give you and your husband a call to talk about the options. I'm sure he'd even let you transfer the payment from the group lessons to private ones."

"My husband?" I asked, startled.

"Well, yeah, if you think the group lessons are expensive, you might be a bit sticker shocked at the cost to invest in private ones."

"I don't care about the cost — I care about quality. And I don't need my husband's approval," I said a little huffily.

"Oh, well, don't worry. When you work with Adan you're going to get quality," he said, trying to placate me.

I had no doubt of that.

CHAPTER SEVEN

ONE ON ONE

Friday was the last day of my group lessons. I decided to try to pay as much attention as I could so that I wouldn't make a complete fool of myself when I finally started my lessons with Adan. I had made Tad sign me up almost immediately after he'd mentioned private lessons, and they were going to start on Monday — three days for an hour and a half a day. Unfortunately, that meant Mo and I could no longer drive together, but she didn't mind too much. She figured that she'd be able to catch a ride with Kane, who was still golfing about three times a week at the same club.

We were going to work on alignment today. This time I had brought a pad of paper for notes, and I planned to study before I met with Adan. I scribbled furiously as I tried to keep up with Tad's lecture: the clubface must be aimed at the target, but must also remain square with

your shoulders, hips and feet. We were supposed to face the club first, then use that
point to adjust our bodies.

Tad illustrated by asking for a volunteer. I
watched as Mo's hand shot up into the air
and he called her in front of the group.
Then, he laid two clubs on the ground
parallel to each other and had her align her
body between them. He handed her a third
club, which she gripped naturally in what
Tad called the baseball grip, and she took a
brisk practice swing out into the field.

The ball went soaring in a straight arc
toward the first hole and landed three
quarters of the way to the green. Tad con-
gratulated Mo on her natural swing and
explained to the others that they would be
spending most of the next week on understanding the fluid movements required for a
solid swing, but for now to remain focused
on grip and alignment.

I gave up taking notes and watched in awe
as each of the other members of our group
took her turn to square her body between
the clubs and take mock swings in the air.
When it was my turn, I somehow couldn't
get both of my feet to stay pointing in the
same direction, and when I took the mock
swing my body went forward with my club
and I tumbled onto the ground. Tad

88

scrambled to help me up, telling me that it was okay, but his eyes betrayed that he'd clearly never seen anyone do that before. He looked very relieved when the lesson ended and he walked over to say good-bye to me.

"Well, Mrs. Edwards, it's been a pleasure. I want to wish you luck in your other lessons. I'm sure that Adan will be able to get you . . ." I think he had wanted to say "up to par," but couldn't quite force the words out.

"Never mind," I said, stuffing my notepad into a duffel bag.

"No, no. Sorry. I just meant that he'll certainly be able to make the most of your skills. Really, you'll be in more capable hands." He looked flustered and embarrassed. "Best of luck to you." He stuck out his hand.

I shook hands with him. He wasn't all that bad, and I *had* almost taken off his head, after all.

As we got close to the clubhouse, I could see Adan leaning against the iron rail that circled the patio, waiting for me. Mo gave me a little shove and disappeared, cutting over a patch of grass toward the parking lot to leave me alone. My heart started to pump double time as I walked up the path. What was the matter with me? I'd talked to hundreds of men before with perfect ease. Why should Adan be any different? I forced a deep breath and let it out slowly. I was *not* going to act like a fourteen-year-old with her first crush. I tried to imagine that Adan was just the manager of any best-in-world business and not just Adan.

"Hello, Adan. I'm glad you remembered to meet me," I said as confidently as I could muster.

He looked slightly taken aback by my sudden poise.

"Mrs. . . . Ren, it's nice to see you again. How was your lesson today?" he asked, waiting for me to enter through the little iron gate and join him at a table he had claimed. The voice threw me off for a nanosecond, but I forced myself to concentrate. *Just another manager, just another manager.* I'd dealt with plenty of intimidating managers before and none could get the best of me.

"How do you think it was? It was just terrible, which would explain the need for the private lessons," I responded. Oops, that came out a little too harsh. Maybe I needed to think of him more as a friend than a manager. That would be better.

A little crease formed between Adan's eyebrows as if he was trying to figure something out, but aside from that he looked almost . . . relieved? That was weird.

I made an effort to take on a friendlier tone. "I'm actually really excited about the lessons. Do you think you'll be able to make anything of me?" I said, as humbly as I could.

Now he looked a little alarmed again. Strange, this guy seemed to relax more when I was treating him with contempt than when I was being pleasant.

"Anyone who has the right attitude, willingness to learn and commitment to practice can learn how to play golf with reasonable competence," he said.

From anyone else it would have sounded like a canned response, but from Adan it sounded like genuine belief in my abilities, no matter how nonexistent or dangerous they actually were. I basked in his assurance.

"Well, that's a relief. I thought I was going to have to take up knitting or something, and frankly it's too hot here to do much with mittens, though I suppose I could always knit you some golf club covers," I said before thinking better of it.

Adan surprised me by laughing. It was such an easy laugh, low and smoldering. It made his blue eyes sparkle like sapphires.

I sat mesmerized by his gaze until he started to look uncomfortable again and broke eye contact.

"You've got a sense of humor," he said, studying the menu and not looking up.

"Yeah, not sure where that came from," I said, honestly.

"Why wouldn't you knit them for your husband?" Adan said in an offhanded manner, but he had looked up and was watching my face.

"What, mittens?" I said. "He's already got more than he can use."

"Golf club covers," he corrected.

"Oh, well, he doesn't really like to golf that much."

This seemed to surprise him. He looked genuinely perplexed.

"I've seen him here every day this week since Monday," Adan said. Then it must have dawned on him that maybe he was breaking some male-golfer code and he covered his tracks. "Or maybe I'm mistaking him for someone else," he muttered and waved for the waitress.

Darn that Andy. Why didn't he just go crawl back under the rock he came from? This was going to be difficult enough without having my fictitious husband dangling under Adan's nose all the time.

"Oh, hello, Adan!" said a chipper voice that broke my meditation. "What can I get for you, handsome?"

I looked up at a fit, little blond waitress wearing a green polo and white shorts. She pulled a pen from behind her ear and favored Adan with a bright smile. *What was it with blonds under five foot five in this place?*

"Actually . . ." Adan was looking at me. "Do you mind if we order lunch? I have another one o'clock planning meeting and I won't have another chance to grab something before then."

"Lunch? Wonderful!" I said with too much enthusiasm. I studied the menu while Adan ordered the broiled salmon salad and an iced tea. I ordered the chipotle chicken salad sandwich I loved so much and a Diet Coke.

"Be right back with the drinks, sweetie," the waitress said to Adan. Before she left, she looked me up and down with little attempt at disguising her disapproval.

"So, you don't wear a ring, I see." He motioned toward my empty left hand.

That was unexpected. I stared at my hand and felt a rush of courage. Should I tell him the truth now?

"To be honest with you —" I said, looking intently into his mesmerizing eyes.

"Yes?" He looked perplexed again.

I chickened out. "It's just too hot to wear it in the summertime. My knuckles swell."

Adan nodded thoughtfully but didn't respond right away. There was an awkward silence that I tried to soften by staring out over the golf course at the stark mountains. The uppity waitress brought us our drinks and I resisted the urge to pull out my Black-Berry and rip on her service.

"You should be careful," he said, out of the blue.

I looked into my Diet Coke to be sure there wasn't a lemon I could choke on that I was missing.

Adan laughed as he watched me.

"I mean about your ring. We get a lot of men on the golf course, and many of them will find any reason to hit on an attractive woman. You'd be safer wearing the ring."

"You think I'm attractive?" The words slipped out before I could stop them. What was *wrong* with me?

Now he looked downright horrified. A lesser man would have stumbled over his next words, but for Adan they came out in complete control.

"Of course I didn't mean myself, Mrs. Edwards. I meant someone who didn't know you were *Mrs.* Edwards."

I watched the bubbles rise in my Coke. Great, we were back to Mrs. Edwards. This was painful. Then, inspiration hit me. If I could get him to relax and feel comfortable around me, I was sure he would open up. What could relax him more than making it perfectly clear that I thought this was a completely platonic visit? What better way than to talk about my husband myself?

"So —" I began, twirling the cloth napkin around in my lap nervously. "*Andy* really seems to like this place. Have you seen him golf?"

It took Adan a minute to understand who I meant.

"Your husband? Yes, he's . . . well at least I think he has . . . been around a lot lately."

"He likes something about this place," I said, smiling.

A dark look passed over Adan's face and he looked at me with a tinge of . . . What was that? Protectiveness? Before I could decide, it was gone.

"Yes," he said cautiously. "How long has he been golfing?"

"Since before we met." There, at least that part was truthful.

"More than five years?" he sounded surprised. "He doesn't usually practice so much, though?" he asked, though it sounded more like a statement.

"Oh boy, is he that bad?" I cringed.

"No . . . No," Adan said.

What kind of a loser idiot did I pick for a husband, anyway?

"He's just . . . out of practice I think. Has he considered lessons?"

"No way," I said, too quickly. "Only one Edwards at a time can afford these lessons, and it's all me."

Adan gave me a captivating smile. "Well, if I had to choose between Edwards, you'd be my first choice." His tone had an easy ring to it now.

Yes. It was working.

"Well if I had to choose instructors, no offense to Tad, you'd be my first choice," I countered.

"Well then, it seems that we are a perfect match," he said. For a split second I thought I saw a slight flush creep up to his ears, but again it was gone in a second. Either this guy was a master at controlling his emotions or I was seeing things.

I let the comment pass, and I prattled on about how nice the weather had been at night lately and how beautiful the view was. His eyes rested on mine and clouded for a second, but he quickly directed them toward the distant mountains and agreed. I asked him a few questions about his job and about how long he'd been in Arizona. Practically everyone was a transplant from somewhere else, so that seemed an easy topic.

"I'm an Arizona native, actually," he said, a smile playing at the edge of his lips.

"No!" I said.

"No, really, I grew up in Tempe and then later attended the university there." He took a bite of his salmon and closed his eyes for a second in appreciation. Ridiculously, that simple gesture sent teensy butterflies flapping against the lining of my stomach and partway up my throat.

"You've never lived anywhere else?" I looked at him astounded, swallowing hard.

"I lived in England for a while, but I returned to Arizona within two years. It's hard to live with the gray when you're so used to a blue sky and bright sun greeting you three hundred and twenty days of the year."

I nodded. I would have trouble moving back to Wisconsin now that I'd had a taste of the desert.

"What did you do in England?"

"My father lives in West Sussex. I wanted to spend some time with him. While I was there I ended up doing some freelancing for the online version of their local paper."

"You're a writer?" I paused with my croissant lifted halfway to my lips.

Adan seemed a little embarrassed. "I try
to be. My degree was in English literature."

"Really?" I asked, almost impolitely.

Adan laughed again. "You ought to try
not to look so shocked. Yes. Golf is not my
first choice in career, but it pays the bills
and keeps me out in the inspirational
outdoors." He looked thoughtfully in the
distance again.

"So you don't write about golf, then?" I
ventured.

"No." He laughed again. "That's one topic
I get enough of during the day. I usually
write about the joy of discovering remote
travel locales."

"You like to travel?" Aside from reading
and my job, traveling was one of my favorite
things to do. "I love to travel."

"Have you been to England?"

"Yes, I went to London for three days
once when I first started my job. I actually
took the Jack the Ripper haunted bus tour
on Valentine's Day. I usually loathe bus
tours, but that one was actually pretty
funny."

"I can think of better ways to spend
Valentine's Day," Adan said.

"Like what?"

"Have you ever been to Ireland?" he said, blushing again and apparently eager to change the subject.

"No, but it's on my list of places to go before I die. Ireland, Australia and Thailand."

"That's a pretty short list."

"I've been a lot of places already." I shrugged.

"Africa?"

"Morocco."

"Ah," he said. "So tell me about your job."

I froze mid-bite. *Did I say something about a job? Think, Ren, think.*

"Oh, um, I worked for an international travel company for a while when I was first out of college, so I got to travel a lot."

"That's explains it. I've met very few people who have been to Africa." He flashed me a beguiling smile and I felt a flush from my toes to my temples. "You must have some interesting stories."

I shrugged again. "Some, but I've still got a lot of ambitions." He had no idea.

"I may be able to help you there."

"What?" I almost choked on a potato chip.

Adan eyed me cautiously before continuing. "Once a year, Desert Fire hosts a golf vacation to one of our sister resorts. That's what all the meetings I've been attending are about. This year we're planning a trip to the Lower Shannon, Ireland. It usually consists of several staff members and a group of about thirty guests. Anyone can go. You and Andy should consider it."

"Andy and me?"

"Sure. You don't need to be a pro golfer — beginners can enjoy many of the courses just as much as anyone."

"Are you going?"

"Just booked my ticket yesterday."

"I'll think about it," I said.

Adan smiled again. "You should — it would be a lot of fun. I know of a few places off the beaten path that I've wanted to visit. I could show the two of you around."

"Oh, well I meant that *I* would think about it. There's no way that Andy could get off of work for that length of time. He's been quite busy," I said.

Adan looked fear-stricken again, and this time the look didn't pass. He tried to casually steer the subject elsewhere, but didn't have much more to say. I could see that some unpleasant thought haunted the edges of his beautiful eyes. I hated seeing it there; I would do anything to wipe that look away.

"So, do you ever visit your parents in England anymore?" I asked, trying to get him talking again.

"I visit my father occasionally, but my mother lives in New Mexico. She moved back there when they divorced."

"Oh, I'm sorry," I said.

"Common story these days," he said somewhat sadly.

"So, your father is English. That explains 'Bennett,' but I haven't heard the name Adan before. Is it a family name?"

Adan shook his head. I noticed that the fearful look still lingered, but I seemed to be doing a pretty good job of distracting him.

"My mother is Spanish. Adan means 'from red earth,'" he explained. "She tells me I was conceived in Sedona." He smiled.

I looked at him incredulously.

"Did I say something?" he asked.

"No," I said. "I just never met anyone else who was named after the color red."

He looked at me questioningly.

"Ren is short for Alizarin. My full name is Alizarin Crimson. Well, it's not spelled correctly, but it's after the red paint color."

The edges of Adan's lips curled up as he considered that. I wished I could read what he was thinking. Whatever it was seemed to have gotten him momentarily to forget whatever had made him uncomfortable earlier.

"What about Scarlett O'Hara?" he said.

"Scarlett O'Hara?" I hadn't expected that.

"She was named after the color red too."

"Ah yes, a kindred spirit for sure, but I've never actually met her, with her being a fictitious character and all." *Though, of course, I could say the same for my so-called husband.*

"Right," he said, a smile still playing on his lips.

"Wait a minute. You've read *Gone with the Wind*?" I asked.

"Sure, twice actually. You?"

"Four times," I responded.

"Why look so surprised?" he asked.

"I've just never met a man who's read the book before — plenty of women, sure, but never a man."

"They don't know what they're missing. Those protagonists named after the color red are really quite engaging." He grinned at me, eyes now clear and bright. He leaned in slightly with a mischievous look.

"You're telling me," I said, mirroring his lean.

He drew back suddenly, looking uncomfortable again. "I've enjoyed talking with you, but I'm afraid I'm going to be late again if I don't get moving." He dug a twenty-dollar bill out of his wallet and stuck it in the leather envelope that held our check.

"I can get mine," I started to protest.

Adan held up his hand to stop me. "I'm about to take a lot of your money for golf lessons. The least you can do is let me buy you one lunch. Besides, I get half off as an employee."

"Thanks," I said, a little guiltily.

"I'll walk with you as far as the lobby," he said, standing to leave. I stood to follow him, but he had stopped walking and was watching someone heading in from across the field. He abruptly turned and placed his hand behind my shoulder to tilt me toward the clubhouse. I felt an involuntary jolt of energy shoot through my arm at the place he made contact. "On second thought, let's cut through the clubhouse, it's quicker."

He swiftly led me up a few stairs and through the inside dining room. I chanced a look out through the French doors as we passed through and caught a glimpse of what had prompted this little detour. Andy was strolling toward the clubhouse with a greasy grin, his arm wrapped tightly around the cart girl.

CHAPTER EIGHT
ZEN REN

When I pulled into the Desert Fire lot on Monday there was a charcoal silver Ducati SportsClassic GT 1000 motorcycle parked in my usual shady spot. The mild tinge of annoyance I felt was quickly overshadowed by my appreciation for that fine machine and the little pitter-patter I felt in my heart when I looked at it.

I chose a spot in the next row back and raked my eyes over it unashamedly while I walked past. I wondered briefly if I could take it with my S4 on the open road, then realized that I was being delusional. I loved my S4, but even it had limits.

When I reached the Pro Shop, Tad's group lesson was already well under way. They were taking swings at actual balls today, and a little camera was set up on a tripod, videotaping them as they took turns. It looked like Mo was up. I gave silent thanks that I had dropped out of the class before they could capture my athletic grace for eternity on tape. I turned toward the shop and called into the open door.

"Knock, knock, anybody home?"

The shop seemed to be empty. I stepped inside and closed the door so no more cool air would escape, and then walked up to the counter. Behind the counter on a low shelf was a black, darkly tinted Ducati helmet. I looked out the window at Tad. He was jogging across the field toward the clubhouse.

"Good morning, Mrs. Edwards," he said, smiling brightly while trying to catch his breath. "Adan said for you to meet him up at the atrium for your first lesson today."

"The atrium?" I repeated.

"It's the first door past the spa reception area."

"Thanks." I must have sounded perplexed because Tad hadn't left yet.

"Do you know where that is?" he asked tentatively.

"Yeah, sure," I said.

"Good. Well, have fun!"

"Wait. Tad?"

He paused at the door. "Yes, Mrs. Edwards?"

I winced at the name.

"Do you ride a motorcycle?" I asked, casting my eyes to the resting helmet.

"Nah, I've got a Mustang," he said. "That belongs to Adan."

Be still my heart.

"Okay, have a good day," I said, my voice cracking.

He looked at me oddly, like he was relieved to have such a nutcase out of his lessons.

"You too, Mrs. Edwards. Good luck."

As promised, I found Adan waiting for me when I reached the atrium. My breath caught at the sight of him. He wore a black polo and beige shorts; his hair looked extremely sexy and unkempt, probably from the helmet. What I hadn't expected was that Little Miss Namaste would be there. Wasn't she in the group lessons?

As usual, she was chattering nonstop to Adan, who listened silently while flipping through a golf handbook. I noticed with some satisfaction that at least he didn't seem to be paying much attention to her. When I opened the glass door to the atrium, a soft whoosh of air caused them both to look my way.

"Good morning, Ren," Adan eyes lit up and he stood to greet me. Karen stayed sitting on one of the lounge chairs, looking unhappy but resigned to my presence.

"Hi, Adan. Hi, Karen," I said. Never let it be said that I lack proper manners. I looked at Adan expectantly. "The atrium?"

"Yes, I thought that we'd start over today, away from the course, and focus instead on the mental aspect of golf."

I looked from him to Karen skeptically, but didn't say anything.

Adan laughed. The sound caused my heart to flutter.

"Don't look so nervous — we're not going to hurt you. I've asked Karen to join us for this lesson because of her expertise in relaxation. Can I get you anything before we get started?"

I shook my head.

"All right then, you take this seat near Karen and I'll sit on the other side of you."

I stepped up to a soft, beige chaise separated from Karen's chair by a large, potted sago palm. I sank stiffly into the chair and heard Adan chuckle again as he took his spot in the chair directly next to mine.

"Try to relax, lean back and close your eyes."

I leaned back in the chair until I was almost horizontal. Before I closed my eyes, I noticed that the ceiling, made of a dimly tinted glass, let in just the right amount of gentle sunlight and no glare.

"Good, Ren. Now breathe deeply in and out . . . slowly." I heard his velvety voice command.

I breathed, unable to deny him his wish. I felt a little of the irritation I had felt at seeing Karen lift from my body.

"Now, we're going to start with a relaxation technique, and then I'm going to teach you some visualizations. Karen?"

Karen's voice cut in high and shrill compared to Adan's. Funny how I hadn't noticed that during the yoga class.

"Rin, I want you to —"

"Ren," Adan corrected her in a low whisper.

A pause ensued, during which I pictured Karen looking annoyed. I smiled to myself.

"Ren," she continued. "I want you to imagine that your body is made of lead, and to begin relaxing each muscle group one at a time. Start with your toes. Your right toes are feeling relaxed. Breathe slowly. The toes are relaxed. Now your right ankle. Breathe slowly. Take your time. Feel how heavy those toes feel . . . just like lead."

Give me a break. I had learned this technique in "How to Avoid Road Rage 101" the first time I'd gone to traffic school after getting snagged on Scottsdale's infamous photo-radar. How much of my money was this chick getting?

"Ren, you don't look relaxed. I want you to focus on breathing."

Ugh. I tried to concentrate. The sooner I relaxed and did what she said, the sooner I'd get to hear Adan's voice again. I listened to Karen drone on until finally she got to my jaw muscles. I resisted the urge to jump up and shout "Yes!" so relieved was I that Karen was going to stop talking soon.

"Now. Your whole body is limp, heavy, filled with lead. Continue to breathe deeply and try to hold on to that feeling," she said.

"Thanks, Karen," I heard Adan whisper. "I'll take it from here."

"I don't mind staying," I heard her whisper back with a slight pleading tone.

"I've got it," he repeated. Commanding.

I heard the cushions in Karen's seat fill up with air when her body left the chair. It was such a pathetically small sound that I was reminded of how very tiny she was. I reminded myself to cough or something when it was my time to get up from the chair.

"Now, Ren, are you feeling relaxed? Nod once if you are."

I nodded once and let out a massive, contented sigh. It was to his credit as a professional that he didn't laugh at me. I flushed slightly anyway.

"Good. I want you to let that feeling overtake you while I talk you through some visualization. Try to picture my words . . ."

I pictured his words, those lucky dogs, getting to roll around on his tongue and pass through those perfect lips.

"Continue breathing, slowly, Ren."

Oops.

"Now picture yourself standing on a pristine, short green lawn that stretches endlessly in front of you. It's a beautiful, sunny day and the sun is warm against your skin. You can feel it on your face and your arms and the top of your head. It's warm, but not hot. It radiates energy and you feel energized by it."

He paused for a moment and I did feel that sun on my skin. It made me feel all tingly inside.

"Good. You can smell freshly cut grass as your feet sink into the short lawn and take root there. You're planted in the grass and it feels completely natural. You can sense your feet providing support for your entire body. You are unmovable from that spot, yet your body feels light and limber.

"Someone hands you a golf club and you wrap your hand around it . . . Ren, I'm going to fold your hands together and lay them on top of your chest now. Just keep breathing and imagining the warmth of the sun and the smell of the grass."

I felt Adan's warm hands grasp mine and gingerly link the index finger of one hand with the pinky finger of the other, then position them low on my chest. It felt exceedingly intimate and I couldn't help letting out the tiniest sigh. Actually, it was more of a moan. I hoped that Adan hadn't noticed.

When Adan started talking again his voice sounded more gravelly than it had at first. He cleared his throat gently and the smooth tone flowed again.

"You've got the club in your hands and the grip feels like you're shaking hands with an old friend. The club feels like a natural extension of your own arms. Can you feel that?"

"Yes," I croaked.

"Good. You're doing great, Ren. Now you notice a little white ball resting on the grass in front of your feet. Your toes are pointing right at it. You feel nothing but peace looking at it."

"Peace," I said.

"Good. You aren't going to hit the ball yet, but you want to take some practice swings. You coil your upper body very slowly backwards. You can feel your spine rotating with the movement. At the same time your arms are swinging up and back so that your hands are above your right shoulder. Then you swing them smoothly down and forward.

"When you arms swing forward, your chest twists to face the field, and you feel your body weight shift to your front foot. It feels like one fluid movement: rotate, swing back and up, and then swing forward and out. Nothing has ever felt so easy or so natural to you before. Again . . ."

Adan took me through about ten practice swings while I listened obediently and tried with all my might to feel what he was telling me to feel. I didn't want to let him down.

"Good. Now step up to the ball . . ."

Oh no, what if I miss? He'll be so disappointed!

"You feel nothing but peace and confidence."

Get a grip, Ren!

"You know that when you swing at this ball, your club will hit it flush and the ball will soar over the field towards the tiny flag you see in the distance. There is no doubt in your mind. Are you ready, Ren?"

"No, I need help." I struggled to make the words surface.

"You're in a safe place, Ren. You have no doubt that you can hit the ball."

"No," I said, abhorred by the panic in my voice, but unable to help it.

Adan paused, apparently trying to decide what to make of my struggle.

". . . Need help," I insisted.

I listened to the sound of Adan's breathing, trying to decipher if he was becoming agitated at all, but it sounded very calm and deep. Another minute went by as we breathed in silence.

"Okay, Ren," he said, starting again. "I'm here to help you. I'm there with you and I know you can hit the ball. You're not alone."

"Where are you?" I asked.

"I'm standing off to the side. I'm watching you and I know you can hit the ball."

I shook my head. "Closer . . ."

More silence.

"Closer . . . Need help," I repeated.

"I'm standing right behind you." I felt Adan's voice low in my ear. "I'm here for you, and I know you can do this."

"Help?" I asked. Even to my own ears my voice sounded weak and pathetic, but hey, I was getting into this visualization thing.

I was amazed that Adan's breathing never betrayed any impatience with me.

"All right, Ren, I'm standing close behind

you and my hands are on the club too. We're swinging it together, and it feels very natural."

"How?" I pressed.

Pause.

"I have my arms around you."

"Oh."

"I have my arms around you, and we're swinging the club together. You and I both know you can hit the ball, and when you do it will soar effortlessly toward the hole."

"Okay." I was feeling a little dizzy now and in no position to argue. If he said we were going to hit that ball, I had no doubt we were going to do it.

"Swing on the count of three, Ren. One . . . two . . . three."

I sucked in a breath of air, picturing the tiny ball flying gracefully over the green lawn like a tiny bird with wings, gliding toward the little flag.

"We did it!" I yelled, my voice sounding suddenly loud and too excited for the little atrium. Mortified by the outburst, I clamped my hands over my mouth and opened my eyes to a squint.

Adan leaned over me, studying my face with a troubled expression. He met my eyes and looked suddenly abashed. Rising quickly he walked to a small table where he'd left his book.

"Well, I think that's enough visualization for one day."

"I didn't do it right," I said, disappointment edging into my voice.

The troubled look on Adan's face melted away and encouragement replaced it.

"Not at all — you were just fine. I realize that visualization is not always the most orthodox place to start a golf lesson, but I wanted to give you some confidence and try to get you to forget what you experienced in the group lessons. I apologize if it was uncomfortable for you."

"I wasn't uncomfortable," I said, too quickly.

Adan looked at me for a long moment, as if trying to decide whether or not to say something he obviously wanted to. He decided not to.

"Good, well, great." He cleared his throat. "That should be enough to help you recall confidence when you need it out on the course. You might try to practice it at home between lessons too."

Was he giving me permission to fantasize about him?

"I'll try to find the time," I said, smiling. "I can't believe all our time is up already."

"Time flies when you're absorbed in an

enjoyable activity," he agreed.

"Yeah, absorbed," I said. "So, I looked into the Ireland trip, and I decided to go."

Adan's face appeared serious. "Just you?"

"Sure. I told you that Andy was too busy to get away."

Adan narrowed his eyes into two slits.

"Don't worry, I don't expect you to babysit me. I know I'm not good, and I won't cramp your style," I assured him with sincerity.

"You couldn't cramp my style, and besides, it's two weeks away. You'll be as ready as any other beginner. I'm just surprised that you decided to go alone."

"I won't be alone. You said there was a large group going, right?"

He nodded thoughtfully. "What about your friend Mary Jo?"

"No, her husband wouldn't let her away for that long."

"But yours has no qualms about it?"

I thought his tone sounded a little critical, but his face was unrevealing.

"No, I think he enjoys a little time to himself once in a while. It's healthy for the relationship."

I wanted him to relax again. He seemed so tense all of a sudden and I was surprised to find that it pained me.

Adan didn't respond, but I thought I perceived his head shake from side to side just a fraction.

"I'll walk you out," he finally said, not meeting my eyes.

I decided to wait for Mo's lesson to finish so that we could go out to lunch and talk. I had to check out a new upscale sushi restaurant for Affluence, and I was just dying to talk to Mo anyway.

I waited for her in one of the plastic chairs outside the Pro Shop, and watched as Adan headed out alone to the driving range opposite it. He grabbed a bucket of balls and began smashing his club into ball after ball with unwavering precision, each one rocketing across the field as straight as an arrow. I watched his back muscles flex under his thin shirt and the way his arm muscles bulged when he brought his swing back. He managed to look completely at ease with his swing, but I could see that his jaw was clenched.

I shivered, hoping I wasn't somehow the cause. Maybe my ineptitude was more annoying than I knew, and I was going to spoil his trip, in spite of his assurances. I resolved to make as many acquaintances as I could on the trip and not monopolize Adan's time. Just because I was starting to feel like I couldn't bear to be away from him didn't mean that he couldn't enjoy himself. I thought about the upcoming trip, and vowed to tell him the truth about my so-called husband if the moment presented itself, then to let the chips fall where they may.

Mo showed up fifteen minutes later, looking flushed and very pleased with herself.

"I think I'm really getting the hang of this golf stuff."

"I'm impressed," I said in agreement. "I can't even manage to hit the ball by myself in my imagination."

Mo looked at me with a puzzled expression.

"I'll explain at lunch," I said, smiling.

"Sorry, honey, I'm not free for lunch today." Just then, Kane and two other men walked up behind Mo. I flinched when I saw who it was. Kane was quick with the introductions.

"Hi-ya, Ren! How's it going? This is Frank and Andy."

"Nice to meet you," I mumbled under my breath to both of them.

Kane looked at me with the same puzzled expression Mo had worn a second ago, then shrugged and turned away.

"Ready for lunch, gorgeous?" he said to Mo.

"Sure am. Just give me a sec, will you?" She cast her eyes in my direction.

Kane nodded in understanding and started to head to the clubhouse with Frank. To my horror, Andy stayed where he was and plopped into the plastic chair beside me, draping his arm around my chair. Who *was* this guy?

"Ren, wow, that's a sexy name. I've seen you around," he said in an oily voice.

I gave him a look that would have sent most men tearing away with their tail between their legs, but Andy didn't seem to get it.

"Nice place, isn't it?" he said, allowing his eyes to travel over the view around him.

I followed his eyes, then rested mine on Adan, who had just finished his first bucket of balls. He looked like he was going to call it a day when he spotted us sitting together. He then grabbed another bucket of balls and turned his back to us.

I sighed with unconcealed impatience.

"Right, fabulous, I've got to go now. Mo?" I stood up and started walking in the direction of the clubhouse. Mo fell into step beside me.

Andy followed like a magnet. "Maybe you

and I could get together sometime?" he said.

Mo threw her arms up in disgust and strode away, obviously trying to keep herself from saying anything that would cause Kane any trouble.

I stopped in my tracks and glared at him with as much icy intensity as I thought it would take to get through his aura of ignorance. Then I pointedly looked down at his finger and picked up his left hand. Ew, it felt like clammy deadweight. "I don't 'get together' with married men," I said, practically shoving his ring in front of his face.

He shrugged and grinned. "Can't blame a guy for trying."

"Oh, yes I can." I stormed off after Mo leaving him standing there with a dumb expression.

"So, what's the deal with Karen?" I asked Mo when I caught up to her. "She skipped your lesson today."

"I heard from Casey, who was very thrilled to have more of Tad's attention to herself, that she only comes when she doesn't have to work. She's apparently just auditing the classes for free when she can."

"Lovely. Well, she showed up at my private lesson."

"What?" Mo looked surprised. "Oh, honey, you'll have to dish later — I want to hear all about it." Then she looked at me with a tinge of pity. "I'm sorry to leave you alone, but Kane's taking some time out for lunch today. You could join us if you wanted —"

"That's okay, I'm going for sushi. Call me later on tonight," I said, letting her off the hook.

"Nice move with Andy," she said, winking at me.

"The pleasure was all mine."

"Ren?" She paused and looked at me like a mother hen.

"Yes?"

"Order the burger this time, will you?" she said.

I laughed at her and walked to the parking lot. As I passed the Ducati, I felt an unexpected stab in my chest. Guilt? I tried to ignore it and slid behind the wheel, then gunned my Audi out of the parking lot and down Scottsdale Road toward the sushi restaurant.

As I passed an empty dirt field, I watched a long, thin dust devil form in the center of the field and edge toward the road, gathering intensity as it passed over the lifeless, dry earth. That's how I felt, like a whirling dust funnel of emotion: guilt, longing, loneliness and jealousy. I didn't like it. I was definitely going to tell Adan the truth while we were in Ireland, so I could get on with my life one way or the other.

In the meantime, I was going to try to focus on my work. I was going to cram as many pleasurable experiences as I could into the next two weeks, even if it killed me. I needed to keep my mind off the man who was quickly becoming more central to my thoughts than I ever could have imagined.

CHAPTER NINE
CLOSE CALL

Tuesday morning dawned blistering hot. So much for the brief reprieve in the weather we'd had the previous week. At least I'd get to wear my Dolce&Gabbana linen, belted sundress while out shopping on Affluence Index business. I was planning to spend the better part of the day making shamefully impractical purchases at an upscale, outdoor North Scottsdale shopping center. With all the focus on golf recently, I'd been slacking.

I showered and dressed at my leisure. I wanted to look my best today. Wearing all those sporty, collared shirts and golf cleats was becoming a little irksome; I was beginning to feel like Kane's boss too. I was definitely going to be looking for some sexy new shoes to remind me that, although I may be a little too tall and a smidgen too clumsy, I was still undeniably female. Every time I thought of Adan, I was reminded of that. Hmm. Maybe I should pick up a few pairs of Lucky jeans for the trip to Ireland too. It couldn't hurt.

I had to circle the boulevards on the perimeter of the shopping center three times before I was able to slide into a parking space, very narrow and much too close to the SUV next to it. I eyed the SUV menacingly, bidding it not to ding my door on the way out, and then I trotted off to leave such matters in the hands of fate.

My first stop was mostly personal, though of course Affluence was paying. I ducked into a quirky little specialty gadget shop and veered in the direction of the travel section. Going on a trip always made me want to purchase some of those mostly-useless-but-just-in-case types of items. I bought a portable, wind-defying umbrella, a twelve-in-one multitool thingy and an iPod charger. Then, although I didn't need it, but because I was feeling altruistic, I bought myself a clip-on book light so that I could read on the plane without disturbing whoever was sitting next to me. The guy at check-out, who was at least ten years younger than me, ogled me appreciatively when I made my purchase. I swear I didn't let it influence my review too heavily.

The next stop was for the jeans. I slid into the adjacent shop and forced myself to look overwhelmed and confused. I needed a good customer-salesperson interaction to even out the other straight purchases I'd made. It didn't take long for a girl in her early twenties to come over and assist me. By the time I had squirreled away three new pairs of Lucky's we were on a first-name basis, and she was assuring me that my new pair of jeans gave me a booty that rivaled Jessica Simpson's when she was on a low-carb diet. That was really saying something, but of course I believed her. Salesperson or no salesperson, my new young friend wouldn't lie to me.

By the time I had finished with my travel accessorizing two shops later, I was feeling parched. A hundred-plus temperature will do that to a person fairly quickly, even in fashionable Scottsdale. I decided to park myself for a brief rest on a bench near one of those fountains that shoots water out of the ground to the rhythm of music. I needed a moment to get my bearings and determine where I might like to have lunch.

I retrieved a map of the shopping area from my quilted handbag, unfolded it and spread it on my lap. I was torn between Tommy Bahamas Tropical Café and the Ocean Club. Both sounded cool and breezy and lovely. I was visualizing myself delving into a pristine shrimp cocktail when I caught a flash of movement near my elbow. A moment later, the three shopping bags I had set on the bench next to me disappeared in a blur, and I heard the pounding and scraping of tennis shoes bolting away. Some thug had stolen my bags, and my booty-loot was in one of them!

I yelped and leapt up to chase after him. As I tried to cross the square, my kitten heel caught the edge of the slick fountain area, and I fumbled with my remaining bags and went sliding, flat on my bottom, across the tile. I skidded to a stop, spread-eagle and stunned, somewhere near the middle of the fountain, just in time for the music to go into the *William Tell* "Overture."

I was immediately surrounded by erupting bursts of water, which mercilessly pelted me, soaking my hair and dress. I think my mouth must have still been open from my attempt to yell after the perpetrator, because I received a full gulp of frigid, chlorinated water for my efforts.

I straightened my skirt as I tried to ignore the bewildered stares of the other shoppers, but abandoned all attempts at dignity when a spurt of water darted straight up my dress. I threw off my shoes and slid out of the fountain in my bare feet.

Before I reached the edge, a firm, steadying hand grabbed my upper arm and eased me forward. I looked up through dripping bangs to thank the kind stranger for taking pity on me, and my heart caught in my throat. It was Adan.

"Are you all right?" he asked, scanning me from head to toe, but not releasing my arm.

"Yes, you are," I said. "I mean, *I* am . . . now that you're here. Where did you come from?" I cringed at my own ineptitude at sounding cool and collected. Oh heck, who was I kidding? At the moment I was one step up from a drenched rat. I was only glad I'd skipped the mascara today or it'd be running down my face faster than the color was creeping into it, which was pretty fast.

"I saw what happened. That looked like a nasty fall," he said, not quite answering my question. "Are you sure you're not hurt?"

"Well, my dress is certainly ruined," I said without really caring. I looked curiously at my arm, which Adan was still absently clutching. My blood was starting to pulse electrically under the spot.

"That's the beauty of living in the desert — give it five minutes and it'll be as good as new." He grinned. "I'm glad you're not hurt."

"Oh! My other bags — that man ran off with them."

"He didn't get far," Adan said, chuckling.

"What do you mean?"

"I told you that I saw what happened. My dog, Orion, has him corned in a doorway a half-block away."

He jerked his head in the direction of one of the smaller side streets leading out from the square. I could see that a snarling mastiff had a man in a hooded sweatshirt pinned against a wall. The man was twitching anxiously, looking for an opening to bolt, but the dog wasn't budging. My shopping bags were lying on their sides a few steps beyond the dog.

"You shop with your dog?" I asked, nonsensically, unable to quite put two and two together.

Adan had appeared from nowhere, in the middle of one of Scottsdale's finest shopping centers, with a large and obviously protective dog, and he had rescued me from humiliation and from losing my Lucky jeans. Actually, to be fair, he was too late for the humiliation, I'd done a pretty thorough job of that before he'd gotten there. The rest was true, though a little overwhelming. A random thought struck me and unfortunately slipped out before I could squelch it.

"Were you following me?" I asked.

Adan laughed and released my arm. My skin protested and flushed with the imprint of his hand as if trying to hold on to the memory.

"Maybe we'd better get you something to eat and drink. You're not making a lot of sense."

I nodded in agreement. "Oh, but I can't go anywhere looking like this," I said, looking at my dress which, though almost dry already, was now crumpled beyond restoration.

"I know of a place. If they'll let Orion in, you'll do. Let's get your bags first. Stay here."

He strode off to where his dog was waiting faithfully, and scooped up the shopping bags just as a security officer in a little white golf cart motored up. Adan said something to the foiled robber, then to the skinny man in the uniform. Finally, he leashed his dog and strode back to me.

"Do you want to press charges with the local police?" he asked.

"Maybe later," I said.

He laughed again. "It's now or never. Although I don't think that guy will be eager for a repeat performance anytime soon."

"I guess I'd better stick around," I said. I must have looked pretty dejected, because Adan tilted my chin up with his index finger and pinned me with those amazing eyes.

"Good choice. Can I still take you to lunch later?"

"Definitely!" I said, far too brightly for someone who'd basically just been assaulted by the chic cousin of a garden hose.

We waited far away from the fountain, in the shade of a skinny palm tree, for the police to show. When they arrived, Adan meandered off to let Orion drink from the fountain while I gave my statement. The police took my name and address, and I was glad that Adan had given me some space — this would be a bad way for him to find out that I wasn't a "Mrs." Edwards, after all. When I finished with the officers, I rejoined Adan and Orion.

"Want to put these in your car?" he asked, holding out the bags to me. He eyed the label on one of them and raised his eyebrows in question.

Ugh! It was from an upscale baby-and-maternity boutique. I'd popped in to check out an adorable shoulder bag that had looked nothing like a diaper bag when I saw it through the window, and on the way out I'd impulse-purchased a little pacifier pod. I had thought that Mo would get a kick out of it. I mean, who needed a pacifier pod? I still wasn't even exactly sure what it was.

I looked up at Adan. No way was I going to let him think I was both married *and* pregnant!

"Baby shower gift," I mumbled. Averting my eyes, I grabbed the bags and headed to the lane where I'd parked my car.

Twenty minutes later, we were seated outside under the cool spray of a mister system at a very *un*fashionable Chinese restaurant. I bit into the sweet-and-sour pork and licked the excess sauce off my lips. Nothing had ever tasted so good. I set down my fork to force myself to pace the meal and watched Adan over the rim of my iced-tea glass. He was skillfully working the chopsticks to down a good portion of the shrimp fried rice. My heart started to pound a little against my breastbone. This was definitely someone I could fall for, and fall hard.

Adan looked up at me.

"Everything okay?" he asked.

"Better than okay," I said. "Tell me, how did you catch that guy so quickly? I didn't even have a chance. Are you a superhero or something?" I asked, only half-joking. He could easily be my superhero.

"Hardly. To tell you the truth, I had spotted him a few minutes earlier, and I was watching him. It was purely coincidence when he targeted you."

"Do you moonlight as an undercover cop?" The thought struck a chord of terror in me. If he did, then he no doubt knew what I was up to.

Adan laughed again. The sound caused a flock of tiny, chirping bluebirds to swirl about in the back of my head.

"No. Like I said, it was coincidence. I did think it was odd that the guy was wearing a hooded sweatshirt when it was a hundred and ten degrees outside — even if he was hanging around the water fountain."

I nodded thoughtfully. That made perfect sense. So it was just a happy coincidence that the hoodlum had accosted me. And now I got to sit there with Adan, talking about exciting things like attempted robbery and treacherous water features.

"So you're off on Tuesdays?" I asked, trying to shift our conversation so that it wouldn't remind him of me sprawled on my rear in a public fountain.

"Not usually, but I'm going to be putting in some extra hours over the weekend to help plan the Ireland trip, so I decided to take some comp time. You're the only one who has private lessons booked at the moment. Most of the others won't start until well into snowbird season."

"So, are most of your private lessons with little old ladies, then?" I asked, comforted by the thought that, at least compared to his regular fare, I was possibly something a little more alluring.

"Mostly, except for Karen."

He shoveled in a mouthful of pork and chewed thoughtfully. I inhaled and sputtered on a lemon seed.

"Are you all right?" Adan asked, concern etching his features.

"F-f-fine," I gasped, struggling for a clean gulp of air.

Adan was halfway out of his seat when I waved him back. I turned a color brighter than the shrimp, but not because I couldn't breathe. I took a large swallow of my tea.

"Really, I'm fine now."

Adan eyed me skeptically, as if I were a living time bomb.

"I promise not to have any more near-emergency situations for the remainder of the day," I assured him.

Adan relaxed a little and took a swallow of his own tea.

"So, Karen?" I said, in what I hoped sounded like a casual, disinterested tone.

"She's really something, huh?"

I watched Adan closely; he seemed to consider that and shrugged in agreement.

"I suppose. How do you mean?" he asked.

"Oh, well — thin, beautiful, sexy," I offered.

He seemed to be contemplating the words, not agreeing, but not actually contradicting me either. Hmm. "So, is she any good?" I asked.

Adan visibly flinched and spluttered a few drops of his own tea across the table before he could catch them with a napkin. "What on earth do you mean?" he asked, eyes wide with reproach.

I made a show of wiping a drop of tea off my bare shoulder. *Interesting response.* I wasn't sure what to make of it.

"You know, is she any *good?*" I leaned over the table toward him, stressing the word. He looked suddenly tense. "At golf, of course. What else would I mean?"

Adan's shoulders relaxed, but his eyes remained wary.

"I wouldn't know," he said deliberately, implying more than he was saying. "She dropped out after only a few days to take up the group lessons. But I give her a few pointers occasionally when she comes by . . . which is rather often lately, now that

I think about it."

"Really?" I asked, feigning innocent surprise. "Why do you think that is?"

Adan looked at me with a steady gaze; it felt like he was burning a slow hole into my facade. He obviously suspected that I was playing some kind of game with him, but clearly didn't know what to make of it.

"What do you think of your hero?" he asked, pointing down under the table to change the subject.

Wow. That was unexpectedly forward. I raked my mind, trying to think of an appropriate response. Should I tell him now that he actually was sort of a hero to me? That the marriage thing was all a farce?

Adan cocked an eyebrow at me.

"My dog?" he said, clarifying.

I looked down at Orion, who was nuzzling my soggy heel. At that precise moment, his long, warm tongue lashed out and licked the bottom of my foot where the now-stretched-out strap of the shoe exposed me. I gave a short and embarrassingly unsophisticated squeal, then gave in and started laughing.

"Oh. He's very affectionate," I conceded. "I think he likes me."

"Naw, it's probably just the wet leather he likes," Adan contradicted.

"No, it's definitely me. I'm wearing Coco Chanel behind my ankles. It's a well-known fact that all dogs love Coco Chanel. It drives them absolutely wild." I smiled, playing along.

Adan's face became serious for a moment.

"You wear perfume behind your ankles?" he asked, clearly intrigued.

"Only when I'm out of liverwurst," I said, grinning. Orion was now in a full-fledged licking frenzy, which had me on the edge of my seat and giggling like a schoolgirl.

"You'd better be careful. Once he attaches himself to someone, you can't ever get rid of him," Adan's eyes sparkled at me.

"Oh well, as long as he's had his shots and knows how to retrieve shopping bags, I could get used to him."

Adan looked down at Orion, amused, then became thoughtful. Finally, a serious, sort of conflicted look settled on his features, replacing the happier mood.

I sighed. So close, yet so far. It looked like we were back to square one. Or would that be hole one?

It certainly wasn't a hole in one.

I couldn't wait for Mo's help to analyze my lunch with Adan, so I called ahead and had her wait for me in the apartment.

"What did you say this thing was, again?" Mo asked, from the spot on my couch where she was working the little flap on the pacifier pod.

"I think you are missing my point," I said, acting slightly annoyed. "It holds pacifiers," I added, by way of explanation.

"I thought that's what the daddies were for," Mo said.

"So the daddy holds the pod that holds the pacifiers. Who cares? You didn't tell me what you think about what I told you about Adan."

"I really doubt that you could get a dad to hold this thing. It's a bit frilly, you know. They prefer to carry diapers and stuff in a manlier-looking bag, like a gym duffel, or a lawn-and-garden garbage sack. How much did you say you paid for it?"

"It was on sale for ninety-nine dollars. It's too small for diapers — it's only meant for pacifiers."

"Still . . ."

"Why are we talking about the pacifier pod? I want to know what you think about what happened with Adan."

"Geez, you're the one that bought the thing."

I gave Mo the glare that said she was approaching dangerous territory. She was in danger of irritating me to the point where I might not buy her another treat should the opportunity arise, even if it was something as odd and generally useless as a pacifier pod. She immediately became focused. Mo sometimes liked to have fun at my expense, but she drew the line at potential loss of freebies.

"So . . . you were saying?" She propped herself up on one elbow.

"I wanted to know what you thought about my conversation with Adan today. Why do you think he was so elusive about Karen?"

"Maybe he's not accustomed to discussing his love life with old married women."

"I am not old!" I objected.

"Ah, but you are married as far as he's concerned. He probably thought it was weird discussing it with you."

"He's not in love with Karen," I asserted.

"How do you know? They're both attractive, single adults. They work together. They sometimes even play together."

"They do not play together," I insisted.

"I meant golf." It was Mo's turn to roll her eyes at me. "They could easily have hooked up."

"I don't believe it. He didn't act interested in her. He seemed almost embarrassed when I implied that there might be some-thing there," I said, pondering the conversation at the restaurant.

"If you don't think they're together, then why would you imply that they were?"

"So that he would deny it, of course."

"Did he deny it?"

"Not exactly. He changed the subject, so I'm thinking he must not want anything to do with her."

"Perfectly logical." Mo eyed me skeptically. "At least it is if you're a *three-year-old*. Did you ever think that maybe he just wants to keep his private life *private?*"

"Of course not," I said, pulling a pint of ice cream from the freezer and grabbing two spoons.

"Of course not," she repeated.

"Right. We're becoming friends, and you open up about things like that with friends," I countered.

"Like you open up about *your* private life?" Mo said, defying my logic.

"Well, that's different," I said, guiltily. I handed her a spoon and plopped down on the couch next to her.

"Uh-huh."

"Did I tell you that he has a really cool dog?" I asked, eager to change the subject.

"Yeah? I love dogs. What kind?" She pried

the lid off the fresh carton and licked the residual ice cream off the bottom of it.

I looked at her reproachfully through squinted eyes.

"What? You weren't planning to save this?" she said with mock surprise. "So, what kind of a dog?"

"A mastiff, I think," I said, trailing my spoon around the rim of the opened ice cream container.

"Mastiff. Nice dogs. Loyal," Mo said, "you know, as in *trustworthy* — like in *honest?*" she probed. "You've heard of that, haven't you?"

I would have loved to have agreed, but I was much too busy cramming my face with *Chocolate Therapy.*

CHAPTER TEN

FORE!

There was a golf cart parked in front of the Pro Shop when I approached it on Friday. I recognized Adan's golf bag in the back and another, smaller bag with women's clubs. I crossed my fingers that they were for me and not for Karen. As I neared the door to the shop, I heard low voices arguing. I froze in place when I heard what they were saying.

"Come on, Tad, you can do this one thing for me," Adan's voice sounded irritated.

"I'm not qualified," Tad stoutly refused whatever it was.

"Don't give me that — you were practically begging for the job two months ago when Karen first arrived."

"That was when I thought she preferred the private lessons. Though it's no secret that her tastes are starting to change back," said Tad, sourly.

"Be a professional," Adan countered

brusquely. "What difference is it to you?" I couldn't tell if he was referring to Karen's preferences or to the favor he had been asking.

"A great deal of difference, thank you." Tad's voice was almost defiant, and I could tell from the shadow that cast through the open door frame that he was making some gesture wih his hands. It looked like he was rubbing his head.

"You don't understand." Adan's voice now sounded almost anguished. I felt another pang in my chest as I listened. *I have to keep away from her.* He said the last words extremely slowly and through obviously clenched teeth.

"Who?" Tad, as usual, was a step behind in understanding.

Adan groaned and said something that sounded like it was causing him so much torture he could barely whisper it. I could make out only the end portion, and it sounded like "ren."

Ren? Or *Karen?* Which did he say? And what did he mean that he had to keep away? This was either very good or very bad. I leaned in closer, but Tad's stubbornness not to cave in to whatever it was that Adan wanted put an abrupt end to the conversation. He came barreling through the door and almost knocked me down.

"Oh, hey, *Ren,*" Tad said a little loudly. "Have fun out there today."

So it was Ren today and not Mrs. Edwards. I burned with curiosity, but it was clear there was no way to ask about their conversation without admitting I'd been eavesdropping. Maybe I could get Mo to snoop around later. She had an uncanny way of getting information out of unsuspecting men, and Tad seemed an especially easy target.

"Hey, Tad," I said.

"Ren," Adan said, blocking the doorway with his body. He looked a little surly.

"Good morning," I said hesitantly.

"Good morning, Adan!" I heard a singsong voice call. *Karen.*

I eyed Adan carefully but his demeanor didn't change. He wasn't giving anything away today.

Happily for me, after Karen had uttered a few words of sickeningly sweet small talk to Adan, she reluctantly veered off and joined the rest of Tad's group, which was already on the green practicing their putting.

I stared after her with thinly disguised irritation.

"I thought we'd start with some observation today," Adan said, indicating the cart.

"There's a good mix of handicaps out on the course today, and I thought that we could critique their swings before we practiced your own."

"Okay," I agreed. *Anything you say.*

Adan's mood improved somewhat as we drove in the cart through the open field. He no longer looked surly, only completely neutral. The temperature was relatively mild, and several fluffy, white clouds dotted the horizon like little cotton balls.

I inhaled a long, deep breath of the tantalizing air and let it out slowly. The action seemed to unsettle Adan. He breathed slowly through his nose a few times before resuming his blank expression.

"Nice day," I said, trying to lighten the atmosphere.

Adan nodded in agreement.

"Wonder if it'll stay cool for the rest of the season or creep back into the hundreds."

Adan didn't answer right away, then only said, "It *is* September."

"Yeah, but I remember that last Thanksgiving it was in the high nineties. That was brutal. But maybe we'll get lucky this year."

"We're here," Adan said, stopping the golf cart sharply.

I flew forward in my seat, and Adan's arm shot out to keep me from crashing into the console. I absently grabbed his arm to push myself back. He recoiled slightly from my touch.

"Thanks," I said timidly.

"My fault — I'll warn you next time." Then he was out of the cart and heaving the bags out of the back, carrying them both, one over each shoulder.

I followed as quickly as I could, having to jog a little to keep up with him.

"Adan?" I called after him.

He stopped partway between me and the group of golfers he was trying to reach.

"Did I do something to upset you?" I asked, unable to bear his coldness any longer.

His face softened slightly as he looked at me. Then he carefully composed his facial features into a look of utmost professionalism.

"Forgive me, please. I have a few things on my mind. I shouldn't have let them impact our lesson. I apologize." He waited for me to catch up with him before setting out again, more slowly this time.

"Want to talk about it?" I offered. "I'm a pretty good listener."

"No." The word was terse but he quickly found control of his voice again. "Thank you, no, it's a private matter. See those golfers out there?" he said, obviously trying to change the subject.

He pointed at a party of three golfers, all older men. I nodded, squinting at them through the sun.

"Those guys golf here every Wednesday, and at other courses throughout the valley the other six days a week. They're fully dedicated to improving their game, and they represent a fairly wide variety of skill. I thought we could learn something by watching them for a bit."

I nodded obediently and stood in silence while the first golfer set up his tee.

"That's Tom. He's one of the best. Check out his follow-through."

I watched as Tom took one practice swing, then sent the ball flying three hundred feet through the air. He looked like he was performing a ballet — only the toe of his back foot was touching the ground when he had finished, and the shaft of his golf club was resting gracefully along the back of his neck.

"Wow," I muttered. I noticed that Adan was equally engrossed in watching.

"That's Hugh. He's not as strong a golfer as Tom, but he's no hack. Watch him line up the ball. Can you see the angle of his clubface to the ball?"

146

Adan was immersed in watching Hugh set up so that he could give me a blow-by-blow account. I took a few steps closer so that I could see better. Hugh swung the club, and the ball swept through the air, landing about twenty yards short of Tom's.

"Chris is next. His alignment isn't perfected yet, but he has a hell of a powerful arm," I heard Adan whisper behind me. I inched closer to get a better look. I noticed that I was casting a shadow across the tee and quickly stepped to the side. There. I remembered at least one thing about golf etiquette.

The movement of my shadow caused Adan to snap away from his observations. When I glanced at him, he seemed to register where I was standing. His face fell aghast, and then two things happened simultaneously: I saw Adan rush toward me with his arm outstretched, ready to pull me back, and from the corner of my eye I saw Chris take a swing. I thought the swing looked pretty, like the flapping of a large bird's wings. Then all went completely silent and black.

"I checked him in this morning — try the clubhouse. Go find him *now*," I heard Adan's voice command through the blackness. I couldn't make out what the person said in reply, but I did hear Adan's response. He must have been leaning directly over me. "Fine, then ask Tiffany if she's seen him," he said, his voice very low and dangerous.

"The medics are here," I heard a woman's voice say.

"I didn't even see her standing there. I should have seen the shadow," a distraught man said.

"She's my best friend — let me see her!" I heard Mo panicking in the distance, a million miles away.

"We've got her now," another man said as I felt my body being lifted by four pairs of strong hands onto a stretcher.

"Can I come with her?" Adan's voice sounded pained.

"Are you family?" a nondescript voice questioned back.

Adan must have shaken his head.

"I'm sorry. We're taking her to Mayo. You can meet us there, if you like."

"Ren . . . I'm sorry," I heard Adan's voice break from behind me as I was carried away.

It's not your fault, I wanted to shout. *Don't leave me!*

But then I felt a throbbing in my right temple that drowned out even the words in my own head. It was like my skull wanted

148

to burst open to release the awful pressure, and I couldn't think of anything else.

When I awoke the second time, I could hear the steady beeping of a machine beside me. I realized I was strapped to something in the bed, not that it was necessary. I had no desire to move even a centimeter at this point. I slowly forced one of my eyes open.

The piercing light was brutal, even though I could see that the shades were drawn. Adan was sitting on a sterile-looking leather chair in the corner of my room, his head in his hands. Tufts of his disheveled black hair stuck out through his fingers. Someone else entered the room then. It was Tad accompanied by a nurse in surgical scrubs. I let my lid fall shut and felt the strain disappear.

"Only two visitors allowed at a time, and we have someone very anxious outside to see her," the nurse was saying to Adan and Tad. "This young man has something brief to tell you. Then one of you can leave. I'm not leaving that poor, distraught soul waiting out there any longer than I have to," she said.

I heard squishy footsteps leave the room. The nurse. Then, Tad's voice cut through the beeping a little too loudly. "Sorry, but I just want to tell you what I have to say then get out. Hospitals make me nervous."

Adan shushed him harshly. "Just keep it down, she has a head injury. The husband's outside?" I heard him say.

What? No, wait, no! I wanted to shout but couldn't even find the energy to open my eye again.

Tad murmured something that was unintelligible to me, and I heard Adan speak again. "Are you sure?"

"Positive, man."

"Then who's out there waiting?"

"Her friend Mary Jo — that chick is ready to wrap a golf club around someone's neck if she doesn't get to see her soon. I had to pry the putter away from her."

Adan seemed to consider whatever it was that Tad had told him. I could hear the chair squeak as he got up and crossed the room. I could feel his presence hovering over me, and then I felt the gentlest caress as the back of his fingers trailed across my chin. Then he was gone.

The next minute I felt a more agitated presence over my bed.

"Ren?" I heard Mo's voice plead. "Ren? Come on, honey — blink, or lift a pinky or something if you can hear me."

I felt the corner of my lip turn up slightly as I tried to smile and tell her I was fine.

"Oh, thank goodness!" she gushed tear-fully. "You gave us such a scare! Okay, honey, okay . . . I'm going to let you rest. I'll be right over there in that chair."

I wanted to ask her about Adan. Was Adan all right? I wanted her to go to him and tell him that it wasn't his fault. I heard Mo sink into the leather chair in the corner, then the squishy footsteps of the nurse again. She fiddled with something near my IV, and a few moments later I felt a heavy, calming sensation wash over me as I drifted back to sleep.

The next time I woke it was night, or else very early morning; it was still dark. I could make out that a figure sat in the chair in the corner, and I smiled. Good old Mo.

My head was still throbbing terribly, but I could at least open my eyes now without feeling splitting pain. I saw that someone had placed a unique arrangement of color-ful sunflowers in a glass vase next to a glass of water on the table beside me. I tried to prop myself up on one elbow to reach for the water, but the room started to spin.

"Mo?" I called out weakly.

A figure appeared instantaneously at my bedside, but it wasn't Mo. I was stunned to see that it was Adan.

He put his hand to my back and helped

me lean forward, then silently handed me the glass. I drank deeply, I was so thirsty that I drained the glass in a matter of seconds.

"Easy there. Feeling better?" he whispered into the darkness.

I tried to nod, but when I tilted my head forward the pain rushed back.

"Careful, I'm going to help you lie back down." Adan's hands were surprisingly gentle as he laid me back against my pillows.

"What . . ." My voice cracked as I spoke. I sounded like a stranger. I tried to clear my throat, and it came out a little closer to normal. "What are you doing here?" I asked.

Adan looked embarrassed. He stared down at the ground. It was so dark that I couldn't see his face clearly.

"What time is it?" I managed.

"It's almost five A.M. I stopped by on my way to the club. But you haven't been alone all night. Mary Jo just left, and —"

I looked at him expectantly.

"You've been in good hands," he said simply.

What did that mean? Had I heard him say earlier that the beast Andy was here? He wouldn't have dared come in and pretend to be my husband here, would he?

"What's wrong with me?" I said slowly.

Now I could see Adan smile. It wasn't a happy smile — but a relieved one.

"Very little, fortunately. You took a sharp slice to your right temple. You were actually lucky that Chris injured his elbow recently, or the force behind the ball that hit you could have caused more damage. As it is, you have a slight concussion." His voice softened then. "I'm really sorry that I put you in harm's way. That was unforgivable."

"No," I squeaked. "It wasn't your fault."

He smiled a sad smile, but didn't otherwise respond. I suddenly felt very tired again and closed my eyes. I thought I felt something warm and soft brush against my cheek before I heard heavy footsteps leave my room, but I couldn't be sure.

CHAPTER ELEVEN
IRELAND

Adan called me every afternoon the following week to check on my recovery. It had been a long week of doing too much of nothing, so I was thrilled to be returning to Desert Fire on the upcoming Friday. I wanted to join Adan for the last day of my lessons before we were supposed to leave for Ireland.

In the meantime, I was condo-ridden. To pass the time, I read. I couldn't focus as well as usual, so instead of re-reading some of my favorite classics, I'd been venturing into some pretty steamy romance novels.

At three-fifteen the phone rang. Even though it was the expected time, it still startled me. The book I'd been devouring practically vaulted up over the back of the couch. I was at a particularly anxious juncture of the story: the hero was about to proclaim his love for the heroine under a worn horse blanket in the back of a cozy carriage, and I was deeply engrossed in the scene. I snapped the book shut and willed myself to breathe normally. "Hello?"

"Ren? It's Adan. Did I catch you at a bad time? You sound like you had to run to the phone."

I felt myself blush horse-blanket red. "No, I can talk."

"How are you feeling today?"

"Great. Perfect. Very healthy. How are you?"

Adan laughed. "I'm just fine — thanks for asking. So, you still think you'll be up for lessons the day after tomorrow?"

"Absolutely," I said, without hesitation.

"I just wanted to make sure. You're missed around here."

I'm missed? Did he mean *he* missed me? My heart thumped and I tried to sound causal when I responded. "I miss . . . being there." That wasn't exactly what I'd wanted to say, but close enough. "Don't start without me," I added.

"I wouldn't dream of it," Adan said smoothly.

I basked silently in the sound of his voice. "Ren?"

"Yes?" *Yes, my love?*

"I'm going to let you get back to Andy, but I'll see you Friday."

Andy. "Andy's not here," I said too quickly.

"He will be soon. I just saw him leave."

"Oh," I said, forgetting to conceal my disappointment. "Well then, I'll see you Friday."

"Do me a favor and let someone give you a ride. I don't like the idea of you driving with that injury."

I knew I was lucky to have gotten away with such a mild injury, but I was pretty much back to normal now except for the occasional headache and an annoying inability to sleep straight through the night. That left me with way too much time to think, mostly about Adan. Right now I was thinking about how sweet it was of him to be concerned for me.

"I'll think about it," I conceded to make him feel better, though I had no intention of giving up my S4 for one more day.

"Right. See you Friday. Be good to yourself."

I will if you will. "See you Friday."

When I arrived at the Pro Shop, I was unpleasantly surprised to see Adan in conversation with Andy, of all people. They were in the office behind the counter, so I couldn't hear what they were saying, but Andy looked a little embarrassed. On the

156

contrary, Adan looked completely composed, almost intimidating. He handed Andy an envelope, then shook his hand with a dismissive air. Andy, looking bewildered but not unpleased, stuffed the envelope into his golf bag. "Weekends only," I heard Andy say before he shrugged and made to leave.

I had quickly ducked back out and stepped aside so Andy could pass. He walked out of the door and down the path toward the main exit so quickly that he didn't even notice me. I waited two minutes, then stepped through the doorway into the cool air of the shop and closed the door behind me.

Adan's face lit up with obvious joy when he saw me, and I realized that I might have underestimated his guilt. He rushed out from behind the counter and took one of my hands in two of his and held it gently. I felt a buzzing in my ears that had nothing to do with my concussion. "Ren, welcome back. How are you feeling?"

"I feel great, thanks."

"No lingering headaches?"

I shook my head. "Nope. It's just the insomnia that bothers me the most." I tried to ignore the tingling in the fingers of the hand he was holding.

"Are you sure you're up for this today?"

"Absolutely," I said, Though truthfully, I was dreading going back out on the course. I was a natural disaster at golf, and people were starting to get hurt. True, so far it had been mostly me, but still.

Adan gave my hand a warm squeeze and the tingling in my fingers burst into outright pulsing.

"We're going to take it very easy, so don't worry," he said. His eyes told me he meant it. I'd be safe with him.

"If you say so," I said.

"I thought maybe we could talk about Ireland."

"Talk about Ireland?" I repeated.

This was too good to be true.

Adan explained. "I thought you might not be too anxious to get back to the mechanics of golfing, and I don't think it'll make much difference in preparing you at this point anyway, so why not enjoy ourselves a little? I won't charge you for the lesson, of course."

"The money doesn't matter so much," I said.

"Something tells me Andy would feel differently," he said, watching me closely.

I wondered again what he might have said to Andy earlier. Maybe Andy had been trying to get compensation for my injury. I wouldn't put it past the weasel.

"I really don't think he'd mind," I reiterated. I was getting ready to tack on that it wouldn't matter to him one bit, because he had nothing to do with me — that it had all been a farce that had gotten wildly out of control — but Adan threw me off guard again.

"Think he'd mind me stealing his wife away for the afternoon?"

"Stealing me away? T-to where? The clubhouse?"

"Actually, you may think I'm a bit corny, but I was thinking that we could hit the bookstore and browse through some of their travel guides. I know all about the golf courses we'll be hitting and a few of the planned tours, but haven't had much chance to think about any of the other local sights. Maybe we could even pick up a classic or two for reading on the plane. My copy of *Gone with the Wind* is pretty dog-eared."

I stood with my mouth partially open, blinking at Adan. I was awed by his sensitivity. "That sounds perfect," I finally managed.

"Great. Let's go." He was still holding my hand with one of his when he reached over the counter and grabbed his helmet from the shelf.

We strolled side by side, past the clubhouse and out to the lot. It should have felt awkward to be walking with hand in hand with Adan in public, because I suspected it wasn't something that a married woman should do, but it felt so right. It was like I could feel the warmth of his palm radiating up my arm and encircling my heart.

I focused on not becoming too light-headed as we entered the parking lot. I didn't want him to think I was feeling ill when what I was really feeling was a rush of dizzying affection. Fortunately, Adan didn't seem to notice. He stopped in front of my Audi as we made our way across the lot.

"Nice ride," he admitted. "But do you mind if I drive? I'm still a little concerned about your head."

"Oh," I said, looking nervously at his Ducati.

"Have you ever ridden before?"

"Sure, lots of times," I told him truthfully. "Both my mother and my father had Gold-wings when I was growing up. Not exactly the same thing, I realize. . . ."

"More or less the same. Your husband won't mind?"

I shook my head soberly. I wanted to tell him, but if I did, he'd probably call the whole afternoon off, and I so desperately wanted to spend some time with him.

"Then hop on." He handed me his helmet and straddled his bike.

I hesitated.

"Nervous?" he asked.

"I'm afraid I might pass out just from the thrill of it — it's so *beautiful*," I confessed.

Adan laughed. The sound made my heart skip.

"I think you can handle the stimulation." An alluring grin spread across his face.

I threw one leg over the seat and settled onto the hard leather, and then I circled my arms around Adan's waist. I felt his solid stomach muscles twitch. I suddenly doubted that I could handle the stimulation. He started the engine anyway, and the bike growled and vibrated between our legs. He eased us out of the spot to the exit.

"Hold on tight," he said.

I pressed my body against his back and closed my eyes and pretended that I was in heaven. The bike lunged forward with such force that I was thrust backward in the seat, in spite of my grip on Adan. The resistance lasted only a second. I opened my eyes as we flew up the road like a missile. Nothing before had ever felt so completely invigorating. I paid attention to the road so that I could lean into the turns as my father had taught me so many years ago. I could see

Adan smile in approval. The only downside was that the ride didn't last long enough; too soon we were at our destination, and I had to dismount.

"Nice," I breathed appreciatively when my feet were back on the ground. I knew a giddy grin was plastered on my face.

"Just 'nice'?" Adan teased. "I expected at least a 'Wow.' Maybe some swooning."

"Wow," I said, and faked a swoon. Adan's arm shot out to steady me and I smiled.

"Skip the swooning," he said. "You're still a little too unstable for comfort."

"I told you I feel perfectly fine."

"Still, I'm keeping an eye on you."

Well, okay, if you insist. He wasn't going to get an argument from me.

He guided me into the bookstore and we found a little corner table in the area that served coffee. We unceremoniously dumped our belongings, then went to peruse the travel section. We returned with an armful of books on Ireland, ranging from heritage to pubs. Adan had brought a steno pad, which he flipped open to a blank page.

"Where to start?" he mused.

"Well, where exactly will we be staying?" I asked, unfolding a travel map.

"In Limerick County at a stunning golf resort in the village of Adare. It's a great base to many of the sites of the region."

"You've been there before?" I asked.

Adan shook his head. "Not exactly. I did once visit the Cliffs of Moher on a day trip, but I've never actually stayed in the Lower Shannon before."

"The Cliffs of Moher? Sounds like something from J.R.R. Tolkien."

"You read fantasy genre?" Adan asked, looking as surprised as I had when he'd told me he'd read *Gone with the Wind*.

"Only the classics," I said. "Tell me about the cliffs."

"They're spectacular. Look." He flipped open a picture book to a page that showed a staggered wall of reddish cliffs extending out over a misty sea.

"I definitely have to go there," I agreed.

"The resort is arranging a tour bus to go there, and also to Bunratty Castle."

I grimaced.

Adan laughed. God how I loved his laugh.

"Not a tour-bus kind of girl?" he asked.

"Not even close. I'd rather pick my way through a map of tiny unmarked, squiggly lines than sit on one of those monstrosities. You miss all the really good stuff on a tour bus."

"I happen to agree . . . which is why I rented a car, myself."

"Smart move," I said, upset that I hadn't thought of doing such a thing.

"I'd be happy to share," Adan said as he watched my face.

"Really? Are you sure? Those rentals are usually about as big as a rolling ice chest. You don't mind me tagging along?" When did he get so comfortable with me? He must really feel bad about that accident, I thought.

"I'll definitely reserve a spot for you for the Cliffs of Moher. Beyond that, you may have to fight with the others. Tad has already tried to corner me into taking a side trip to Dublin."

"But that's nowhere near where we're staying," I protested.

"You have to remember that the Republic of Ireland is relatively small. If you were visiting Scottsdale from out-of-state, would you consider a trek to the Grand Canyon?"

"Of course. I see your point," I said. But I was a little disappointed that Adan might be traipsing all over Ireland with his buddies. I probably wouldn't get to see that much of him.

Adan was closely watching my face and looking . . . amused? Well, that was an improvement on pained, panicked, or surly.

"So . . . who else from the resort is planning to come?" I asked.

"No one from your old group lesson, but a bunch of people from the weekend lessons and a few more from out of state, mostly repeat visitors to the resort. They always receive a special invitation since they're somewhat loyal to us."

I nodded. Customer loyalty I understood.

"Are any other staff members going besides you and Tad?" I tried to sound nonchalant. *Not Karen, please, not Karen . . .*

"Sure. The general manager and his wife, the clubhouse manager, a bunch of the support staff . . . no one I think you know except for maybe Karen."

Darn. I'd known this was too good to be true.

"Oh."

Adan seemed to sense my disappointment.

"Almost everyone will spend the majority of time golfing. I plan to have a little more balance in my days, though I am dying to get you out on Lahinch. You're going to love that."

"Lahinch?"

"It's one of the most amazing golf courses in Ireland. I've always wanted to play it. We'll have to play Two-Man No Scotch or something, so you don't feel any pressure."

"Right. Two-Man No Scotch. Sounds like a plan."

Adan looked amused again. "It means we each tee off, then switch balls — playing each other's ball where it lies. It's a good game for beginners."

"In other words, you'll be playing both our games of golf for us."

"Not at all."

"I like it," I said, smiling. "The best of both worlds."

"I see it that way too," Adan said.

I cast my eyes down at my tour book. Was Adan actually flirting with me? How had this happened again? I should probably reiterate that I didn't consider the accident one speck his fault — but I kind of liked the flirting.

"So," I said, gazing at the book. "See anything you like?"

When Adan didn't respond, I looked up and found him staring at me with a wicked look on his face. "Without a doubt."

My cheeks burned and I had to cast my eyes down again. Yikes! He *was* flirting. Only . . . Wait a minute . . . If he thought I was married and he was still flirting, wasn't that a major character flaw? And if I flirted back, what did that make me? I had chastised Andy for flirting with me, but if Adan was willing to flirt with a married woman then was he really the man I dreamt that he was?

"Tell me what you're thinking." Adan broke into my thoughts, still watching me.

No way. "Oh, just that I probably need to get back and get organized. I haven't even started packing yet," I answered.

"We haven't decided yet which books to keep."

"You can pick them. I trust your judgment." Or did I? I watched Adan shuffle through the stack of books and select three of the smallest but more clearly organized. Oh yes, in spite of what my conscience might try to argue, I was completely and unequivocally enamored of this man. If he told me that the right thing to do was to jump off the Cliffs of Moher into the sea, I know I would have a hard time denying him.

We walked back to the Ducati in silence. When we reached Desert Fire, Adan dropped me at my car door. I eyed his bike wistfully as I backed away, but then a thought dawned on me.

"How are you getting to the airport tomorrow?" I asked. "That bike may be beautiful, but I don't see it carrying much luggage."

"I was planning to call the airport shuttle."

"That's silly. Where do you live? I can

swing by and pick you up on my way."

"I don't want to trouble you."

"It's no trouble."

He finally agreed and gave me the address of a condo located in the same fashionable part of North Scottsdale that I had been shopping in the day that man had tried to steal my Luckys. So *that's* why he'd been there. It explained the dog too. He'd probably been out walking the dog and had happened to see me on the bench. I felt a warm rush of affection toward Adan at the memory of how he'd rescued me. Giving him a ride to the airport was the least I could do.

"Six o'clock?" I ventured.

"Thanks, Ren," he said.

When I got home that afternoon, I packed in a frenzy and was so wiped out from the activity and the lack of sleep the night before that I decided to turn in early. I saw that I had four messages beeping on my answering machine, but I didn't have the energy to retrieve them. If it was work, they'd catch me on my BlackBerry when I finally turned it back on, but I'd taken the next ten days as vacation, so I should be clear there — and anything else could wait until I returned. I settled into my bed with a dog-eared copy of *Gone with the Wind,* but never even made it to the first barbecue scene.

I woke up almost twelve hours later. I couldn't believe the alarm hadn't gone off the one day I needed to be on time to catch a flight out of the country. I shook the clock irritably, and it went off. Ugh. After the world's fastest shower, I threw on some jeans and a T-shirt and grabbed a light, fitted jacket from the hook at the very back of my closet. I was grateful I'd retained my old traveling habit of purchasing separate toiletries and makeup from the ones I used every day and keeping them packed and at the ready. Since I'd packed my shoes and clothes the night before, all I needed to do now was to zip up the suitcase and go.

I had exactly five minutes to make it to Adan's. I cursed myself for not having asked for his home phone number. I couldn't even call to tell him I was running late. Oh well, I had my S4. I'd probably make it without any problem at this hour on a Saturday.

I pulled out of my lot and saw a white Volvo just pulling into the opposite entrance. Mo? What could she be doing here? *Sorry, Mo, no time!* She honked wildly at me when I didn't stop. I made a mental note to call her as soon as I got to the airport. She probably just wanted the key so she could use my pool.

I tore out of the lot and headed south. Luck was not with me. I hit every stoplight except the one at the major intersection just before Adan's. I was twenty minutes late pulling up in front of the high-end retailer that Adan's flat rested above. I honked the Audi's horn. I needn't have bothered; he was already waiting in the shadows of the doorway, looking cool and collected in dark jeans and a blue polo with a tan leather jacket. He was the exact opposite of my own frazzled exterior.

"Good morning," he said with an enticing smile. "I heard you tear around that corner. You sure I'm safe in this thing?"

"Funny. Get in — we're late."

"Whoa, you can take your time. The flight's been delayed thirty minutes. We'll get there with a full two hours to spare."

"You're not just saying that so I don't drive like a maniac?"

"Would I lie to you?"

I felt a twinge of guilt at that comment. *No, but I've been lying to you!*

"So, we have time to hit Starbucks?" I said.

"Do you *need* to hit Starbucks?" he asked.

"Oh yes." I rubbed my temple with one hand.

"Then, by all means . . ."

Adan ordered a Venti decaf drip coffee and I ordered my usual Grande nonfat latte. I was amazed at the service — I hadn't been to this particular Starbucks in over six months, and the girl taking my order still remembered my name. I couldn't resist switching on my BlackBerry for a minute and tapping in a few notes as we sat at a small table in the corner. Adan eyed me while I did.

"Urgent e-mail?" he asked.

"Yeah, I needed to get in touch with Mo," I said, feeling horrible that I was lying again, but not knowing how to stop.

"If you mean Mary Jo, that reminds me — she came looking for you yesterday. She seemed pretty intent on telling you something, and she wasn't too friendly."

The first part of his sentence didn't surprise me — Mo considered even the most basic of gossip to be urgent — but the second part did.

"Mo didn't seem friendly?"

"Not to me. She kind of gave me the evil eye."

"Huh."

That was definitely odd, but there was no

time to think about that now. We had to get back on the road. I switched off the Black-Berry. "Ready?"

"You're the boss," he said.

We made it to the airport with the full two hours to spare, just as Adan had said that we would. Sadly, it was the last time I was going to be alone with him for a while; he was immediately flanked by several old-timers, from earlier days at the resort . . . and, of course, by Karen. She wasn't leaving his side.

I followed the group to the kiosks and checked myself in. Adan caught my eye over the sea of his silver- and white-haired admirers. I motioned for him to go on ahead, and veered for the closest ladies' room. Those lattes really went through you on an empty stomach.

When I reached the gate, people were still peppering Adan with questions about the trip and telling him about their recent golf conquests. It was like he was a celebrity. A few times Adan caught my eye and looked apologetic, but I just smiled and held up a copy of *Gone with the Wind,* then dipped my nose into the pages. I'd already read it a half dozen times, but now it reminded me of Adan. Besides, I was determined not to be a nuisance.

On the plane, I noticed that Karen had wheedled herself into the exit row next to Adan. Like she needed the extra leg room! I was stuck between an old man who smelled like cigar smoke and a Goth teenager who was apparently going for the world's record of facial piercings. I was grateful to have my book. I spent most of the trip trying not to stare down the aisle at Adan's leg, which was the only part of him I could see from my seat. Even that was sexy.

When Aer Lingus made its final descent into Shannon Airport, I folded over the top corner of chapter twenty-five and stretched in my seat as much as possible without elbowing Goth-boy and puncturing myself. We'd made only one stop at JFK, so I'd been able to plow through a good chunk of the book. I noticed that I had more in common with Scarlett than a name; she, too, was somewhat conniving when it came to getting close to the man she loved. I didn't care much for that particular similarity.

It was still pretty early when we disembarked. When our party finished with baggage claim, a pretty brunet woman with pale ivory skin was waiting for us with a clipboard. She busied herself arranging people into groups of five to a taxi. I was about to join the last herd when I felt a tug at my sleeve.

"I thought you didn't like traveling with the lemmings," Adan said, looking incredibly handsome and impossibly fresh for having just crossed the Atlantic. He dangled the keys to his rental in front of me.

"Don't be cruel," I said.

"Since when is it cruel to save a damsel in distress?"

"You're saving me?"

"From riding in that smelly sardine can, yes."

"Oh," I said, favoring him with a giant grin. "In that case, I accept. Lead me to your valiant steed."

"Hmm. Well, I think it's actually a Ford Fiesta hatchback."

"A Fiesta, huh? Maybe I should take my chances with the sardines."

"Did I mention I saw the old guy who recycles his socks climb in there?" Adan nodded toward the cab.

"I suddenly feel an affinity for hatchbacks."

Adan picked up my suitcase and smiled. "Let's go, then. The chariot awaits."

I followed Adan across the concrete toward rental car pickup and looked at the sky. It was clear and blue, without a single cloud. I couldn't see much green from here, but I knew it was out there. I could hardly wait.

We passed Karen on the sidewalk; she was just standing there with an unconcealed pout. Adan nodded as we passed but didn't extend any invitations. After all, the car was so small that three would have been a crowd. I couldn't resist peeking over my shoulder to watch her mope off and join the others.

"They do make rolling luggage, you know," Adan said, breaking my reverie.

I looked affectionately at my old-fashioned, hardcover suitcase. Of course, it was much easier to be affectionate about it when someone else was lugging it around.

"Sure, but the souvenir travel stickers don't stick as well to fabric."

When we reached the rental car, Adan had to move his own suitcase out of the back to make room for my enormous, clunky one. He wedged his behind the seat, and then he popped a map out of the glove box and handed it to me. The village of Adare was circled in red ink on the map.

"It's time to test those superior navigational skills," he said.

I glanced at the map. "Piece of cake. They're all major roads."

We followed the "Way Out" signs, and I told Adan to take the N24 to Limerick Road, then to travel south until we passed into the village. I set down the map and watched him. He was driving exceedingly slow.

"Speed traps," he explained, reading my thoughts.

When we settled on the highway, he stepped on the gas, but not too hard. We didn't want to miss the landscape. I couldn't resist asking Adan about why he'd let me ride with him.

"So, how come you're being so nice to me?" I asked warily.

"I owe you," Adan said simply.

"Owe me? For what?"

Adan thought for a minute. The pause seemed so long that it caused me to question whether what came out of his mouth when he finally spoke was what he originally intended. "For being so forgiving about the accident," he said. "I'm grateful that you weren't hurt worse. That would have been . . . unbearable." His forehead crinkled as he thought about it.

I wondered if it was the guilt that he'd have found unbearable or something more. Probably it was just the guilt. He was something of a perfectionist and I'd probably messed up his safety record. "You don't owe me anything," I said. I didn't want him to feel sorry for me — I wanted him to feel something else.

Adan smiled. "Too late. I'm in debt and I plan to make good."

Okay, so I didn't mind the sound of *that* so much. "So I got nailed in the head, and you saved me from the ride from hell. Let's just call it even."

"Okay, then, even." His lips curved up pleasantly, and I sat back to enjoy the scenery. The countryside was picturesque with low rolling hills and lush green pastures. I couldn't think of another place on earth that would be a greater contrast to Scottsdale. I probably could have used the time to broach the subject of my alleged husband, but it was so peaceful that I didn't want to stir up any potential ill feelings. Not just yet.

CHAPTER TWELVE

OH, LOVELY VALE!

The drive to the village of Adare was surprisingly short. In only thirty minutes, we were pulling over the main bridge into town. I had been pretty much pasted to the window since Limerick. We had passed dozens of stone cottages painted in white and yellow. I wanted to take pictures of them all in the early sunlight, but my camera was packed between two sweaters in my bag.

"Oooh, what's that?" I asked, pointing to a gray rectangular stone structure that hovered in front of the road.

"Desmond Castle," Adan answered.

"You've done your research," I said.

"Lots of time to read on the plane." He shrugged.

At least that meant he hadn't been talking to Karen the whole way.

"What river is that?" I asked.

"The River Maigue," Adan said.

"You're a regular guidebook." I grinned, soaking in the cozy feel of this village snuggled in the countryside.

"This is amazing," I said. "Look at all the colors!" The village was filled with closely nestled little buildings, most of them adorned with thatched roofs. I saw pale blues, bright yellows, peach and green everywhere I looked. Hand-painted signs on ironwork scrolls announced the names of restaurants and pubs. Bright bunches of flowers blossomed in baskets situated partway up the streetlamps.

"That's the washing pool," Adan said, indicating a small, triangular body of water with boundaries of masonry wall. "And the entrance to the Manor should be here somewhere."

"There!" I said, indicating a wide arch carved from a tall, gray stone building.

Adan pulled through the tunnel. When the full image of the Manor was impressed upon me, I gasped audibly. Adan watched me out of the corner of his eye. It was a massive Gothic-style structure with perfectly manicured, emerald green lawns sitting majestically beside the meandering river.

"Like it?" Adan asked.

"It's so . . . formidable," I finally said, at a loss for the right word. The truth is, the manor was spectacular; it was by far the most elegant-looking place I had ever stayed. But I couldn't help feeling a stab of disappointment at seeing it. The village of Adare had been so quaint, and this was so . . . *regal.* I realized that I had been hoping for something more personal.

"You don't seem impressed," Adan said.

"Oh, I'm impressed. Who wouldn't be?"

"What is it, then?"

Was I that obvious, or was he that perceptive? I looked at Adan, and he was watching me as he slowly pulled up the drive.

"It's just a bit *too* impressive, if you know what I mean."

Adan narrowed his intense, blue eyes at me and seemed to consider that, and then he smiled broadly. "I think I do, and I have to say, you never cease to surprise me."

"Oh well, we'll get to see a lot of the quaint country when we take that trip to the Cliffs of Moher, right?"

"I promise. Wait here," he said when we pulled to a stop.

"Why?"

"Trust me."

I sighed. I couldn't help but trust him. I used the time alone in the car to study the map. Everything that I wanted to see seemed so close together, but I never was

180

very good at comprehending the scale of things. If I could talk Adan into spending a full day with me, I thought I might be able to see the bulk of what was on my list.

Ten minutes later Adan returned, followed by a tall, thin man with dark hair. The man opened my door, nodded once, then tilted up my seat slightly so that he could pile into the backseat next to the luggage. Adan didn't look happy about it.

"Ren, Richard. Richard, Ren," he said by way of introduction as he started the car and flipped a U-turn back towards the exit.

"Uh, nice to meet you Richard?" I said. It came out sounding like a question.

"Ren — what an adorable name, and aren't you a doll! I can't thank you two enough for taking me with you. I can't believe they sold out the rooms!" Richard said in a musical voice.

I raised my eyebrows at Adan. "We're taking him with us?" I said.

"Oh, you don't mind, do you, love? They said they'd drive me over later with the luggage, but I just wanted to get settled. I'm exhausted from that flight!" he said, fanning himself with his hand.

"Of course I don't mind," I said. "I just didn't realize we were leaving."

Adan opened his mouth to explain, but

Richard cut him off. "What? You didn't hear? Those fools at the agency back in the States overbooked the Manor — apparently there wasn't a single room left except for the staff." He gave Adan a look of disapproval over the seat. "Though at least *this one* was gentlemanly enough to give his room up to one of the *paying* guests. Unfortunately, it wasn't me. So here I am."

I looked at Adan. That still didn't explain where we were going.

"We don't have rooms?" I asked, a little nervously.

"Trust me," Adan repeated.

"Oh we have a room, doll, at another local hotel, though nothing so fancy as this one. I'd better get a refund when we get back . . . but at least it's an adventure, right?" said Richard, almost giddy now.

Adan was looking at Richard like he wished he could stuff him into the hatch with my suitcase, so I decided not to draw him into further conversation. I sat quietly while he drove out of the Manor's driveway and stopped in front of a quaint-looking, brightly yellow-painted building. A sign out front read *The Dunnery Arms.*

We left the bags in the car and walked up to the entrance. My heart skipped a little when we entered and I caught a glimpse of the drawing room behind the entrance. It was painted in pale yellow and furnished with pale blue chairs and sofas. There was a white fireplace mantel with two painted plates resting on either end. Richard looked at me and rolled his eyes as if to silently complain about the step down in accommodations, but I was so entranced by the warm, country atmosphere that I paid him no attention. I noticed Adan watching my expression again as my eyes traveled the room. He seemed pleased by my response.

A matron greeted us with zealous hospitality, and Adan returned her warmth as he explained the situation at the Manor and inquired about rooms. At the same time Adan was speaking to the older woman, two young women who were wearing clothes that were too dressy for early morning waltzed through the door and past our party. One of them poked the other and giggled as she passed Adan, not bothering to hide her admiration. Then they disappeared up the staircase. I felt a little pang of annoyance, but Adan had hardly noticed them.

A few short minutes later we were heading upstairs ourselves, following an exceptionally congenial porter, who had already retrieved our bags from the car and was proudly informing us that their hotel bar was central to the town's entertainment for visitors and locals alike. He stopped partway down the hallway and threw open the door to the first room, setting my luggage just inside the door. Then he did the same for Richard at the next room. Adan's room was on the other side of Richard's. I saw just a flash of irritation cross Adan's face when he contemplated the arrangements, but it didn't last. The charm of the place was so compelling that it defied anyone to be anything but at ease.

"Are you feeling tired?" Adan asked me.

"A little. I think I'll take a short nap, and then I may explore the village." I said.

"If you'd like, we could meet for a late breakfast in three hours. I need to head back over to the Manor to iron out some itinerary details, but not until this afternoon. I hear this place serves an amazing Sunday brunch."

"Mmm brunch — yummy! You can count me in." Richard's voice floated between us.

Adan eyed him. "Sure. Ten-thirty, then?" he said graciously.

After assuring Adan we'd be there, I disappeared behind my door. Adan waited until I was inside before I heard him close his own door. I smiled to myself. This little arrangement was working out okay after all.

I turned to survey my room and had to restrain myself from jumping up and down in spite of my exhaustion. The room was perfect. It was painted in the same sunny yellow as the drawing room, with a bright white chair railing and crown molding accenting the walls. The furnishings looked like comfortable antiques, and a large, framed mirror stood on one wall. I had my own private bath and dressing room, where a luxurious white robe draped from a hook. Matching fluffy white slippers beckoned me from the floor in front of my bed.

Ah, the bed. It looked so inviting, partially covered by a pretty orange canopy and already turned down for me. I shuffled out of my shoes and crossed the room to the bed, not even bothering to take off my jacket before lying down on the crisp, white sheets. I sat up just long enough to set the clock on the bedside table for two hours from now, then pulled the soft down duvet over my body and let my face sink into two layers of heavenly down pillows.

When the alarm beeped two hours later, it took every ounce of willpower for me not to punch the snooze button and pull the cozy covers over my head. Only the thought of

Adan and food could summon me out of the warm cocoon. I rolled out of bed and revived myself under a hot shower, then slipped on a pair of jeans and a sunny, yellow V-neck jersey, to match my mood, before heading to the dining room.

The dining room was absolutely enchanting. It was painted a warm red color and had the same decorative white molding as my room. The tables were covered in crisp white cloths. I spotted Adan and Richard already sitting at one, and crossed the room to join them.

"Well! Good morning, sunshine," Richard snickered. "Where'd you find that shirt, at the Partridge Family garage sale?"

My first instinct was to sneer at Richard, but it turned into a laugh, and I ended up sticking out my tongue at him instead.

"I'm just joshing you, sweetheart. I like it — it matches the décor."

Adan had stood up when I approached and settled back into his seat as I took mine.

"Such a gentleman, this one," Richard gushed.

"You look nice," Adan managed to say over Richard's prattling.

"Thanks," I said, "So, what's on the menu?"

"I'm having the Irish oatmeal," Richard

said. "I get so stopped up on these transatlantic flights, if you know what I mean," he whispered confidentially.

I couldn't help laughing at him. True, he was a little annoying, but kind of like a lost puppy. Clearly, he just needed attention.

"They're famous for their prime roast rib," Adan suggested.

"Well then, when in Adare —"

"I thought you might say that. I took the liberty of ordering for you," Adan said, looking triumphantly at Richard.

"Oh fine, so I owe you a Guinness," Richard said snootily. "Though I consider it no great feat that you know what your girlfriend likes to eat. I just said it wasn't polite to order for her. Most women secretly hate that."

Adan laughed. "Do you secretly hate that?" he asked me.

"I never really thought about it before," I answered honestly. "I guess not."

"Hmmph," said Richard.

"I'm . . . not his girlfriend," I said, my voice trembling a little at the presumption.

"No, that's true," Adan agreed, looking serious again. "She's actually quite happily married."

"Get out!" Richard said, looking at me expectantly.

"It's true," I croaked. My throat suddenly felt very dry.

"So you're unattached then?" Richard said, leaning his elbow in closer to Adan.

"Not *that* unattached," Adan responded.

"Figures," Richard said.

Oh great. Just great. I couldn't tell Adan now, not here with an audience. And what had he meant by "not that unattached"? He couldn't mean Karen, could he? Ugh, why hadn't I come clean earlier? Stupid, stupid, stupid.

"Hello, earth to Ren." Richard's voice cut into my self-berating.

The waiter had rolled the trolley up to our table and was politely waiting for me to indicate what cut I wanted. I chose the rarest cut. Why not live dangerously? I had nothing to lose.

The prime roast turned out to be heavenly. I didn't think anything so tender or succulent had passed my lips in quite some time. I relished every bite, then sopped up the juice with soda bread, closing my eyes and savoring every drop as it passed over my tongue, before I licked my lips in satisfaction. When I opened my eyes and laid down my fork, I noticed both Adan and Richard watching me with slightly dropped jaws and parted lips.

I shifted uncomfortably, cleared my throat and took a sip of mineral water. "Sorry," I mumbled sheepishly. "It was really good."

After Adan and Richard composed themselves and finished their own brunch, Adan rose to leave.

"I've got to go. Tomorrow starts the first day of tours and golfing, and the staff needs to get organized. I'm not responsible for much, but I do need to be sure everyone has the equipment they need and has signed up for tee times. I probably won't be back until late, but I arranged a tee time for the two of us at Lahinch tomorrow. You'll be okay tonight?" He gave me a torn look.

"Of course, I'll be fine. I'll check out the village, and then later the hotel pub."

"Oh, that sounds good, love. Do you mind if I tag along? I don't have anything planned until tomorrow either," Richard asked.

"You bet. See? Richard and I have a date, so you don't need to babysit me. I'll be perfect."

Adan acted as if he wanted to comment, but instead just looked from Richard to me somewhat skeptically, then signed the meal to his room, nodded and left.

"Whew," Richard said. "I like him, but I'm glad he's gone. Too much testosterone at one table — it makes me nervous."

I chuckled.

"Besides, he's drawing all the attention. I feel like the ugly stepsister," he continued.

I looked around the room. Two older couples and a heavy-set, single woman were the only other diners.

"You had your eye on someone?" I teased.

"Not anymore," he said. "Looks to me like his attentions lie elsewhere."

"Adan?"

"*Of course* Mr. Hottie Pants. Don't tell me you don't see it. You'd better be very clear with that boy, or you're going to find yourself in a nasty jam. Being in a foreign country tends to make people forget all the rules."

"I wish," I said.

"Excuse me? You no-likey the hubby?"

"I no-havey the hubby," I said, frowning.

"Okay, sweetheart, spill the beans." He leaned in excitedly, ready to hang on to my every word.

"Well . . . I sort of led Adan to believe I was married before I really knew him, and now that I *do* know him and really *want* to know him even better . . . I've gotten myself in pretty deep, and I'm not sure how to come clean."

"Oh what a tangled web —"

"Not helping."

"Sorry."

"And now that I've told you, it makes it even worse. He's going to think that it was some kind of conspiracy."

" 'Cause there's no danger of that already, huh?"

"Again, not helping."

Richard shook his head in sympathy. "Well, doll, you'd better tell him soon. I believe that man is seriously contemplating adultery, and think of what a rat that must make him feel like, a man with such obvious integrity."

I winced. He was right, of course, but how could I tell him now? I would just have to make the opportunity. I vowed to myself that I'd do it tomorrow.

"Want to go explore?" I asked, changing the subject.

"Absolutely. Let me just grab my bonnet."

I looked at him disbelievingly.

"Tell me you're kidding."

"Of course I'm kidding — bonnets are *so* last season." He rolled his eyes and we stood up to exit the dining room.

I ran upstairs to grab my purse and nearly knocked over one of the women I'd seen entering the hotel earlier that morning. It looked like a painful hangover had finally caught up with her.

"Oh, excuse me," I said. "Are you all right?"

She nodded. "Nothing that a little hair of the dog won't fix, though I'm not sure catching Mr. Lisdoonvarna is worth all of this." She stumbled past me toward the dining room.

I met Richard in front of the hotel and we started strolling to the village center, passing colorfully painted buildings and quaint stone structures on the way. Richard exclaimed enthusiastically whenever something charming caught his eye, which was often.

"Richard?" I interrupted his gushing over a particularly colorfully painted pub sign. "Have you ever heard of Mr. Lisdoonvarna?"

"What, you haven't?"

I shook my head.

"Well, if someone is after Mr. Lisdoonvarna they're going to have to get in line after me. I may not be Queen of the Burren, but there's no denying that I'm some queen." He winked at his own joke. I didn't get it.

"Richard, what are you talking about?"

"The big matchmaking festival."

"Matchmaking festival?"

"It's tradition. For the month of September and during this first week in October there's this huge music-and-dance festival in the village of Lisdoonvarna, not far from here. Singles from everywhere flock there to dance and be merry with each other and to find their Mr. or Ms. Right-for-the-Night. It's really just an excuse for a big party, though I have heard they still have a real matchmaker in town that you can meet by request. He's supposed to be the descendant of the farmers who were real matchmakers in the days of old, or something crazy like that."

"Really? Matchmakers?" No matter what my luck with men, I had never contemplated a dating service of any kind. The whole thing seemed a little trite to me.

"Yes. At the grand finale of the thing they actually even name one lucky man Mr. Lisdoonvarna, and one lucky woman the Queen of the Burren. You know, the Burren is that desolate land mass just northwest of here . . ."

I nodded my head. I'd seen it on the map.

"Anyway, it's all for fun, but it's supposed to be a great place for singles to mingle."

"And the matchmaker actually handles introductions?"

"By appointment only."

"Interesting. What other festivals are there around here?"

"Mostly sporting events, amateur horse racing, that type of thing — nothing that catches my interest so much as a bunch of rowdy singles."

I laughed and pointed out an impressive view from across the bridge. We spent the afternoon pleasantly strolling the quiet streets and occasionally ducking into an establishment that wasn't closed, being that it was Sunday. We had a late lunch of soup and sandwiches at a small restaurant and bar opposite the village park, then strolled back to the pub at Dunnery's before it was dark.

I was halfway through my second Guinness when Adan walked in. Richard winked at me and sidled over to a strawberry blond, baby-faced man at the bar, leaving me alone.

"May I join you?" Adan asked.

"Sure," I said, slurring the *sh* just a little. The jet lag combined with the Guinness had me really relaxed.

"I see you're getting into the local culture." Adan smiled, his blue eyes dancing in the light from the fireplace.

"Mmm," I said, leaning toward him across the table.

"Just remember that we have an early date tomorrow," Adan said, tapping my pint with his index finger.

"Date?" I asked, trying to look directly in his face, but having trouble keeping my eyes open.

"Yes, remember me? Your golf instructor? I made us a tee time for five-thirty so that we could play the links and then have some time for a little tour off the beaten path as I promised."

"A.M.?" I said, missing most of what he'd said after "five."

Adan laughed. "Okay, maybe you should go up to bed now."

"I like the sound of that," I said, then covered my mouth quickly with my hand. "I don't know where that came from."

Adan raised his eyebrows at me, clearly surprised.

"How many of those have you had?"

"Just two." I held up three fingers, I think.

"You should be careful drinking anything until the jet lag settles," he said.

"It might be a little late for that."

"No kidding."

"Did you say something about a date . . . you and me?"

"Yes, Ren, at four-thirty A.M. I'm going to send a wake-up knock to your room and you're going to get into something comfortable and warm and meet me downstairs at five. Then we're going to go *golfing*." He said the words slowly so I could understand.

"Okay," I said, smiling up at him.

"Okay," he said. "Bedtime."

He led me out of the pub and I waved at Richard from across the room. Then I leaned on Adan as we ascended the stairs to our rooms.

"You know, I'm a married woman," I said, trying to give him one of Mo's come-hither looks.

He looked at me intently in the face. "I know, Ren," he said. Then he helped me unlock the door to my room never crossing the threshold.

"Tomorrow, five A.M."

"Good night, gentleman," I said, giggling.

"Good night, Ren."

CHAPTER THIRTEEN
THE BEATEN PATH

Four-thirty A.M. comes awfully early in Adare. I woke up feeling like I had swallowed one of those little pom-pom thingies from the back of a golf sock, fuzzy and dry. I blinked my eyes against the brightness of the lamp and thought about cancelling the date. The date! Adan had said we had a date, and while I'm sure he didn't mean it exactly like *that*, it didn't change the fact that I was going to be spending the whole day with him.

The thought helped to shove away the sleepy haze and buoyed my spirits. As the haze started to drift, I began to remember, with an impending feeling of dread, some of the prior night's conversation. Had I tried to flirt with Adan when I was drunk? Had we talked about my husband? This was not good.

I shuffled into my slippers and to the bathroom. Just as I finished a quick shower, there was a knock on my door. I glanced at the clock; it was only four-fifty — I still had ten minutes. I shrugged into the soft bath-robe and answered the knock. A cheerful waiter rolled in a room-service set for one. A sprig of flowers and baby's breath peeked out of a ceramic white vase and a large pot of steaming coffee sat seductively in the center of the table. The waiter lifted the metal cover of my breakfast and revealed two eggs, sunny-side-up, two slices of bacon, a soda roll with jam and a small pitcher of cream. Perfect. I thanked the waiter, handed him a tip and closed the door behind him, then sat down to eat. After I had finished my breakfast, I dried my hair and pulled on a pair of jeans and a thick, cream-colored pullover sweater over a white T-shirt. I made it downstairs at two minutes after five. Not bad considering the jet lag and the Guinness.

Adan was waiting for me, looking tempt-ing in a pair of gray khakis and a light blue pullover sweater, the sleeves pushed up to his elbow showing his sculpted forearms. His hair was still slightly damp from the shower and formed little ringlets around his collar. I noticed when I stood next to him that he smelled both subtly spicy and woodsy. I inhaled deeply.

"Good morning. How are you feeling this morning?" Adan asked hesitantly.

"Wonderful, thanks to you. The breakfast was a nice touch, thanks." I smiled.

"I thought you could use some substance. We've got a long day ahead of us."

"How long does it take to golf?"

"About four hours for the eighteen holes."

"That's not too bad."

"Then a short drive north for the Cliffs of Moher."

"We're going there today?" I asked, surprised. He hadn't mentioned it earlier, and I was a little afraid that, after he'd kept his promise to show me that sight, he might desert me for the rest of the trip.

"Today's the best day. It's going to be sunny, and there should be fewer tourists — the others will all be focused on golf or the more local sites they can walk to these first few days."

"Okay," I said, knowing it didn't matter. I would follow him just about anywhere, any day of the week, in any weather.

The drive to Lahinch golf course wasn't very long. I started to get nervous when I saw what we were going to be up against. The ground was practically covered in mogul-like dunes, and there was such a strong gale coming from the direction of the ocean that my hair was blowing up and around and flattening against my face.

"You're kidding, right?" I asked, hooking my finger around my bangs and pulling them back so that I could see Adan.

"Don't worry. It won't be as difficult as it looks, the way we'll be playing," he said, placing his ball on the back tee for the first hole. I was amazed that it didn't get blown right off and roll into a nearby fallout.

"I'm not sure about this."

"It's early — you won't have a big audience. Trust me. Two-Man No Scotch, remember?"

Adan made sure I was standing far enough behind him before he made his first shot, which landed nicely up the hill he was aiming for. Then he motioned for me to stand at the front tees. He dug a white leather golf glove out of his pocket and handed it to me. I looked at the glove with unconcealed distaste, but Adan slipped it over my left hand anyway.

"It's tacky," Adan explained.

"You're telling me. I feel like Michael Jackson."

Adan laughed warmly. I felt my toes, which had been feeling a little frosty in the early morning dew, thaw immediately along with much of the rest of my body.

"I mean, it'll help you grip the club more easily."

"Of course you did."

"Now, Ren, I'm going to come up behind you and help you just like we did in the atrium."

"Just like the atrium?" I said, feeling weak-kneed at the memory.

Adan slipped behind me and wrapped his arms around my body, placing his warm hands over my own, which were already gripping the club. He was wrong; it wasn't just like the atrium. It was a million times better. His body felt solid and safe behind me. I felt my heart begin to beat wildly and hoped that Adan couldn't sense it too.

"Ready?" His voice was low and alluring in my ear.

I couldn't speak. I only nodded.

Adan guided my arms backward and up, then forward in one fluent movement, and we made a connection with the ball. He was being so gentle with me that my ball didn't go nearly as far as his had, but at least it didn't plunge into the sheer drop-off that loomed to the right of us.

"Not bad, he said. "I'll play your ball, and you can take mine up the hill."

We played like that for the next several holes, up and down the hummocks and hollows, Adan never leaving my side except to keep at least one of the balls on course. Even though we had never gotten to practice putting, I surprised myself by not being half bad. My semi-competency must have been thanks to all of those miserable first dates on which I'd been subjected to playing goofy-golf in Arizona. When we got to the fifth hole, Adan paused and grinned surreptitiously.

"You're going to like this one," he said.

"Oh?" I questioned.

"The hole is known as 'Dell.' It's only a par three, so you should feel pretty confident given what you just played. It's another blind tee, but just wait until you see what's waiting on the other side."

"More sheer descents?"

"You have to see for yourself, but I can tell you that it's legendary."

We teed off and walked onto the field until we could see the green. It was nestled in a natural sort of amphitheater hidden by dunes on every side, completely private. As usual, Adan helped me with my next swing.

I felt his powerful body radiating heat behind me, only this time after we hit the ball he kept his arms around me longer than necessary. I felt a little shiver of pleasure run down my spine as he lingered there, breathing warmly into my ear.

My little white lie nagged at me. I didn't want him to feel like a rat, but he wasn't really doing anything wrong; he was just standing there, holding me. Still, I knew I should tell him now, but I was afraid to move. Adan wasn't moving either. I lost resolve with every passing second; it felt like my entire body was turning to jelly. If he didn't either do something or pull away soon, I might just slip through his arms and melt into a puddle of pulsing nerves.

"Sorry," I finally heard his voice say, husky but controlled. "I must have been daydreaming. That was completely inappropriate."

"No —" I started to say, grateful to feel my legs again now that he had pulled away.

"Yes, it was. Forgive me." He was insistent. "Let's go. You'll want to see the view after this hole."

We walked past the far dune and I felt the full force of the Atlantic Ocean in my face. It was a slap of cold air that I desperately needed at that moment, sobering me.

I watched Adan as a content-looking smile settled on his lips. He ran his fingers through his thick hair as his gaze danced over the crashing waves. I thought about just telling him the truth right then and there, just

203

blurting it out: *I'm not married. I'M NOT MARRIED!* But my courage failed me yet again. The morning was turning out to be so perfect, I didn't want to be the one to wipe that lovely smile from his face . . . I didn't want him to hate me.

We stood silently for a few minutes, watching the powerful waves peak wildly in the wind. It was a truly breathtaking sight. Eventually, we tore ourselves away and finished the next few holes. By the time we had completed nine, I was exhausted. It had taken longer than expected to play the way we had.

Adan looked me over, then looked at his watch.

"Would you mind if we cut it short and did only the nine?" he asked.

Would I mind? *No, bless you!* "I can make it . . . don't want to ruin your fun," I said, composed.

"Well, considering that you *are* most of my fun, I'd rather have you alert for the rest of the afternoon."

I blushed fiercely. What should I say to that? That was flirting, right? Innocent — but flirting.

"If you insist. I *would* like to see the Cliffs of Moher before dark," I said, deciding that the best tactic was to ignore the first part of what he'd said.

Adan looked at me for a long moment with a steady, searching gaze. I continued to blush. He then smiled softy, gently shaking his head. He grabbed my clubs before setting off for the clubhouse. We didn't really speak again until we were back in the little rental car, driving the short stint to the Cliffs of Moher.

"You don't need me to navigate?" I asked.

"It's only two miles. If I get us lost in two miles on a single road leading up the coast, we're in trouble," Adan said cheerfully.

"More than you think," I murmured.

Adan looked at me expectantly, but I pretended to be studying the landscape. When I didn't elaborate, Adan looked back at the road and started humming to himself. He was in an awfully cheerful mood, I noticed. I decided to forget my embarrassment from earlier and resolved to enjoy his affable company.

As I looked out the window, could see that we were nearing the cliffs. The weather had turned a little gray, and the air was moister than it had been on the links. A fine mist sprayed the windshield. As we drove on, we passed very few trees and the land started to look desolate. It was still green, and there were quite a few plants, but they seemed sort of twisted and out of place, like something from a ghost story. Patches of land revealed flat limestone slabs with only tufts of grass or the hardiest of plants growing between them.

"We're in the southernmost part of the Burren," Adan explained. "It starts to look a bit grim from here on in, even more so up north, but the cliffs are spectacular."

I nodded as I examined his fine profile and the muscles of his arm as he gripped the wheel. As far as I was concerned, we could be driving on the surface of the moon, as long as I had Adan to look at.

Adan pulled the rental to a stop in front of the Visitor's Centre and got out to buy our tickets. We agreed to skip the interpretive center and the virtual reality tour of the cliffs in favor of taking the one-hour hike along the cliffs themselves. Fortunately, Adan had planned ahead and had two pullover rain ponchos and a pair of binoculars in the trunk. I was really grateful for the rain ponchos — there's nothing worse than the feeling of wet wool against your skin.

We passed a weather-beaten sign as we started up the path: *Caution — Dangerous Cliffs Ahead.* I glanced nervously at Adan and he chuckled.

"Don't worry. I won't let you fall."

Too late. I've fallen for you. I marveled at the number of tourists who climbed over the stone wall to get a better look. I was committed to staying on the path and in one piece, and was relieved to see that Adan was true to his word and showed no intention to do otherwise.

The cliffs were a glorious sight: massive, sheer walls of black shale and limestone, shooting up almost vertically from the dark blue, hazy sea. I drew in a sharp breath when I saw them.

"Amazing," I whispered.

Adan stopped walking so that we could take in the view.

"What are those white specks?" I asked.

He handed me the binoculars.

"Birds' nests!" I said, "Imagine living in such a perilous place . . ."

"I can imagine it might be a thrill to live a little dangerously now and then," Adan said.

I drew down the binoculars and looked at him. I had a funny feeling that he wasn't talking about his Ducati, but he didn't say anything more.

When we reached Hag's Head, we turned back and spent another hour walking back north along the cliffs. All in all, we had spent almost three hours at the cliffs.

Exhausted, we headed north along the breathtaking coastal road to the village of Doolin, where Adan promised me a late lunch and some traditional Irish music. The drive was spectacular, both on the west where the coastal waters raged in the ever-increasing wind and rain, and on the east where the Burren was making itself known by the bleakness of the landscape. There were vast quantities of stones, and occasionally we ran across a formation where someone had piled them into a unique tower. I wondered whether they were someone's recent fancy or the work of centuries ago. They looked like they had always been a part of that rugged landscape.

The whole area felt a little eerie, and I was glad for Adan's company. He talked about the sites of the Burren as he drove, trying to get a feel from me for which places I might like to visit later before returning to Adare.

"Aillwee Cave?" I suggested, remembering that the Burren had thousands of caves but only one was open to visitors.

"Nice choice. But are you sure your husband would like the idea of you exploring dark, deserted caves with a strange man?" he asked.

"You're not that strange," I responded

playfully, not really answering the question. "Do you know you can still see places where the bears used to hibernate in those caves?"

He raised his eyebrows at me. I didn't know if it was because I evaded his question or something else.

"I thought I was supposed to be the guide-book."

"I do occasionally read things other than the classics." I grinned.

"Then Aillwee Cave it is. We'll hit it on our way out."

"Won't it be too dark by then?" I asked, though not because I was afraid of visiting the caves at any time with Adan by my side. There were other things I was worried about, like controlling myself not to grab him in the dark.

"Trust me," he said. Then he added, "What else do you want to see while we're out and about?"

You mean other than more of you? I pretended to think for a moment. "Just Doolin," I answered. I was getting really hungry.

By the time we reached Doolin, I was famished.

As we drove down Fisherstreet, I was again struck by the uplifting colors of the buildings. There were no thatched roofs here that I could see, but the village still had its own unique quaintness to it. Several young men and women clad in jeans strolled along the street hand in hand. It was subtly romantic. I glanced under my lashes, Mostyle, at Adan — but he was busy looking for a parking spot.

He found a spot, and we walked toward McDaley's, one of several famed pubs in the area. As we walked, Adan explained about the three brothers who had put the town on the map with their musical talent and distinctive sound. I listened only half-heartedly. I wished we were as carefree as those other couples. I longed to slip my hand into Adan's, but instead I wrapped both of my hands around myself and nodded politely as Adan spoke.

When we entered the pub, there were only three other couples present, along with a table of five rowdy tourists who looked to be well into their third round. A lovely, fair-haired woman in her middle years greeted us with a smile and showed us to a table. Behind the bar, a brawny man kept the beer tap flowing.

Adan slipped in next to me at the corner booth, sitting so close that our thighs touched. I tried to ignore the pulsing sensation in my leg and studied the menu. I ordered the Atlantic salmon, which I assumed would be far fresher than in Arizona, and Adan ordered the Irish stew. We both opted for pints of Guinness. As we ate our leisurely meal and drank the rich Guinness in relative silence, I began to relax. I observed to Adan that the crowd was starting to pick up a bit, and when four men carrying instrument cases entered the pub, we understood why.

"Ah, here we are," Adan whispered into my ear. I trembled as the sound of his words caressed my neck. His voice always did intrigue me.

Adan set down his spoon, took a long drink of Guinness and stretched his arm across the length of the back of the booth.

A tantalizing scent of spice wafted up to my nose. My heart started pounding against my ribcage, and I suddenly lost my appetite for the fish. I set down my fork and sipped at my own beer, trying to focus on the musicians as they pulled some chairs together and tuned their instruments.

There were four men on the little stage, one carrying a fiddle, another a flute, another a guitar. The last man was working with sort of a hand drum.

"That's a bodhran," Adan said in a low, quiet voice, this time letting his lips linger near my too-sensitive earlobe. I quivered as

I felt Adan's warm breath make contact with my skin. Oh boy. This was it.

I knew it wasn't right to encourage him without having told him the truth, but I couldn't manage to pull myself away. I closed my eyes and tilted my head back ever so slightly. I heard Adan's breath quicken at what he clearly considered an invitation, and the next thing I felt were his lips, soft and burning, pressed hard against the side of my neck just below my ear.

I gasped, unable to help myself. He moaned in response and allowed his lips to travel further down my neck. My heart beat furiously and my chest heaved so deeply that I worried I would draw attention. I opened my eyes a slit; no one seemed to notice us, so I let them fall shut again. A lively musical reel startled me, and my eyes flew back open.

The room was dimmer than it had been when I'd first closed my eyes, and it spun drunkenly as I pulled away from Adan.

I opened my mouth to speak, but no words came out. I had no clue what I would have said anyway, and it wouldn't have mattered much — the music was so loud that he wouldn't have heard me. Adan searched my face with eager eyes, as if trying to bare my soul. The look was torturous to me. I felt a stab of agony as I thought about the conflict he must be going through. He was drawn to me, as I was to him. But as far as he knew, I was forbidden. I now wished more than ever that I had told him the truth earlier. But how could I do it now?

We peered into each other's eyes, me with guilt, Adan evidently trying to ascertain some meaning — or maybe just some permission there. Was this really all that wrong? It felt so right. Adan seemed to make a decision, because his eyes cleared of restraint and instead flashed longing and determination. The look terrified and thrilled me at the same time.

The musicians had made it partway through their song when Adan slipped his arm around my waist and slid off the bench, pulling me with him. He dropped several foreign bills on the table and pressed me lightly to his side. Then he swept me out into the darkened, quiet street. Happy notes of music drifted through the open window and floated softy in the moist night air around us.

We walked silently around the side of the tavern, into an even darker alley. A swift look around told us that we were alone. Adan leaned his back against the cracked yellow wall and wrapped his other arm around my waist, rolling my body on top of his and pulling me closer into him. His eyes closed as one of his hands pressed tenderly against the small of my back and the other traveled slowly up my spine, leaving a tingling trail of awareness. It paused behind my neck, and I felt Adan bury his face in my hair as my own eyes closed and I let out a blissful sigh. Adan groaned in response, his breathing heavy. His lips grazed my neck and collarbone before he lifted his head and found my mouth, hot and urgent.

I should have expected it, but the sensation took me by surprise. The kiss caused a violent explosion of feelings within me. He deepened it and the world around me became a vacuum. I leaned into him. Nothing existed but Adan's body pressed against mine.

He tasted sweet, like the Guinness. His lips were soft and warm, but firm and commanding. His hungry mouth worked mine, and I felt myself encouraging him. Every one of my nerves responded to him with yearning. I was lost in his warmth, completely in his power. Nothing mattered but this very moment in time. My ears rang and my skin burned. I shivered with excitement.

Adan pulled his face away, his voice smoldering dangerously. "You're cold." He pulled me closer, not waiting for an answer. He rubbed my arms and back with his burning palms.

I shook my head, unable to speak.

"We should get back to the car," he said suddenly, clearly struggling to regain his composure.

I could neither shake my head again nor nod, so I followed him obediently back to the car. When we were inside he cranked the little heater, and I felt cool air blast through the tiny vents until it slowly warmed and settled into a steady stream. I absently held my fingers up in front of a vent.

Adan sat with the keys in the ignition, staring straight ahead out of the window at nothing. It looked like he was waging another internal battle with himself.

"Look —" I managed to say, my voice cracking nervously. I was going to tell him right now and put an end to this agony.

Adan interrupted me. "I was . . . way out of line back there. I . . . don't know what to say for myself. I know I should keep away from you," he said.

My heart lurched in empathy for what he must be feeling.

"No, Adan, I need to tell you —"

"But I can't," he continued as if he hadn't heard me. "I can't, and I don't want to. I want you." He stared at me intently. "Nothing else matters to me. If I burn in hell for coveting another man's wife, then so be it. Ren . . . tell me you'll spend the night with me in Lisdoonvarna."

What? What did he just say?

"I booked a room for us at a little bed-and-breakfast there. I called last night after putting you to bed. I knew then that I couldn't let another night pass with you in your own bed and me in mine. I *need* to be with you. I *need* to have you, Ren."

What? This wasn't right. I couldn't be hearing him right. Was he telling me that he had decided it was okay to be with me, even though I was married? Was he telling me that he didn't care, that he was going to attach himself to me anyway, integrity be damned?

I stared at Adan openmouthed as his eyes simmered in the darkness. How could this be the man I thought I loved. Yes, *loved*. All the signs had been there — but this was the upstanding man that I couldn't imagine my life without, offering to be the *other man!* A man who gave no serious thought to the sacredness of matrimony? My mind reeled as these thoughts flitted through my head. I glanced again at Adan, and he was watching me closely. He seemed to be . . . What was

216

that? Amused?

I closed my mouth and stared straight ahead without speaking. I didn't trust myself to speak. Part of me felt like I deserved this. I had lied to and betrayed this man, and I had forced him to reveal this ugly blemish in his character. Had it not been for me, might this side of him never have surfaced? My troubled soul felt bleaker and drearier than the cold, wet stones of the Burren.

Adan must have assumed that my silence meant that I was considering what he had said. He pulled out of our parking spot and out of town; then he turned on an inland road that would bring us, in a short jaunt, to the quaint little country room that he had booked *the day before,* for the two of us to spend the night together in Lisdoonvarna. I felt sick to my stomach.

Chapter Fourteen
BED AND BREAKFAST

We pulled up in front of a low fence made of tumbled gray brick. The square house beyond it was made of the same and was surrounded by flowering bushes. Even in the dark, I could see that it was charming. I remained in my seat after Adan killed the engine, so he walked around to my side of the car and opened my door. I looked up at him with a mixture of embarrassment and disgust. No, disgust was probably too strong a word — it was more like immense disappointment. He looked at me soberly and waited. I sighed and stepped out of the car and started walking toward the building, not waiting for Adan. I suddenly felt very tired.

We got an enthusiastic greeting from the female proprietor of the establishment, a stout woman with a dimpled chin and dimpled, pink cheeks and a halo of fine, strawberry red hair. She planted two balled-up fists on her considerable hips, where they immediately disappeared into the patterned fabric, and she studied us through wire-rimmed glasses that seemed too delicate for her hearty frame. After a moment, she nodded approvingly, then indicated for her son, a flush-faced boy of about fourteen, to show us to our room. I marveled that she didn't seem at all perturbed by the fact that we had no luggage. I turned to Adan to protest.

"I didn't bring any of my things," I said, hoping I could convince him to drive back to Adare instead of go through with his immoral plans.

I thought I saw Adan wink at the matron. "I think you'll find everything you need upstairs," he said.

I gave him a puzzled look and paused on the bottom step, unwilling to go up. I felt Adan suddenly behind me. He brushed aside my hair and placed a brief, tender kiss on the back of my neck with his warm, moist lips. I felt my body respond instinctively, then cursed myself and drew up tight. I thought I heard Adan chuckle softly.

"I'm afraid you'll have to go up without me for now. I have some business to take care of. I need to get in touch with the Manor to make sure everyone is situated for tomorrow, and to let them know I'll be coming back late tomorrow morning. I'll be in the drawing room when you're ready for me to come up."

"Ready for you . . . ?" I repeated, feeling slightly nauseated again.

Adan smiled broadly and patted me affectionately on the rear. I jumped forward in shock. What was going on here? I begrudgingly followed the makeshift porter up the stairs and hesitated in front of my room. It seemed the eager boy wasn't going anywhere until I'd entered the room, so I stepped across the threshold and nodded politely to him, then closed and locked the door.

I leaned against the inside of the door and concentrated on not hyperventilating. It was going to be okay. I was a grown woman, and I had time to think now. It didn't sound like Adan was going to come up and ravage me until I invited him to. Given the circumstances, there was no way in God's green Ireland I was going to do that. But what was I going to do? Leave him sitting down there in the drawing room by himself all night? It had possibilities . . .

No, no. I couldn't do that. I scanned the room for a chair where I could sit down to think. I was horrified to see that, along with two robes and two pairs of slippers, there were two sets of clothes lying out on the bed. There was a woman's floral-print cotton skirt and blue wool sweater, and there was a man's pair of slacks and a gray V-neck sweater. Both were patiently waiting to be occupied, as if they knew all along that we'd cave in to our desires. I plunked into the nearest chair, a soft wingback, and raised my fingers to my lips. I'd never been a nail biter, but now seemed as good a time as any to start. When I'd nibbled the nails on my right hand to nubs, I realized I needed a stronger vice, but nothing sprang to mind. Maybe a walk in the cool night air would clear my head and buy me some time. I stood up, walked to the window and glanced down the street. There was some big street party going on with lots of people and lots of drinking and dancing, it seemed.

I turned on my heels and headed straight for the door, tiptoeing down the steps. I stopped abruptly when the porter came out of nowhere to stand in front of me. He looked at me questioningly. I lifted my finger to my lips to request his silence, then cast my eyes toward the drawing room where I could hear Adan talking on the phone.

"If he asks, can you tell him that I was

restless and went for a walk?" I asked, eyes pleading. "I may not be back for a while."

The boy looked confused, but nodded his understanding and stepped aside to let me pass. I opened the front door. A little gust of wind fluttered the lace curtains in the window. I slipped outside and headed for the main street in town.

It didn't take me long to find the action. In front of what seemed like every pub and restaurant in town, there were little groups of live musicians playing their fiddles and flutes while rambunctious singles, mostly foreigners, twirled and danced in the street with beers and whiskeys in their hands. Whiskey. That's what I needed. I walked a little farther up the street, not wanting to duck into the very first bar, lest I be too easy for Adan to find. I finally found a friendly looking pub with wooden booths, tongue-in-groove pine ceilings and hundreds of foreign postcards on the walls. An enormous man with a German accent lifted a beer as I walked by. "Prost!" he said cheerfully, drinking from the pint. Little streams of foam escaped the edges of his mouth.

I ducked inside quickly, bumping up against more foreign men and giddy, flirtatious single women of all shapes and sizes. This was a singles' party all right. At least

Adan would have difficulty finding me amidst this bunch. I squeezed through the crowd and toward the back of the bar. A tall, good-looking but thin man with shocking red hair greeted me.

"Ah, here's a bonny lass!" he said with a Scottish accent.

I looked behind me, hoping he was referring to someone else.

His lanky, curly-haired buddy leaned out from his perch on the barstool behind him and spoke in a heavy Australian accent.

"Aye, she's a dinki-di sheila, all right," he said, raking his eyes over me. "Join us for some Amber fluid, sheila?"

I looked them over. They seemed innocent enough, given the throng of people partying around me. I nodded.

"A whiskey, actually," I said to the stout man behind the bar. He nodded and disappeared.

"Straight whiskey, ay? I hope you're not a screamer," the Australian said, looking at me skeptically.

"Excuse me?" I said.

The first man responded, "He means a lightweight drunk. Better watch yourself around here if you are . . . or if you want, we'll keep an eye on you," he said in perfect American English, while trying to assess my figure under my bulky sweater.

"You're American?" I asked, ignoring the visual groping.

"Yeah, I've had a bit to drink," he admitted. "My accent changes depending on who I've been talking to. I've never seen this many people from all over the world in one place before."

"Where are you from?" I asked.

"New York," he said.

I rolled my eyes at him, then turned back to the bartender who had returned with my whiskey. I grabbed the glass and threw back the burning liquid. It stung the back of my throat, and when I swallowed, a little line of fire traced down to my belly. When I stopped coughing and sputtering, I tapped the empty glass on the bar.

"Another please," I said.

"Up for ripper of a party, eh?" the lanky one said.

I turned to the redhead, waiting for the translation.

"Looking for a wild party?" he dutifully said.

"Drowning sorrows is more like it," I said despondently.

"What's a gorgeous chick like you have to be sad about on a night like this?" the American asked. I tentatively sipped the next whiskey, not wanting to perpetuate the wild-ripper-of-a-party theory, then set the glass on the table, glaring at him.

"One guess," I said.

"Boyfriend?"

"Something like that," I mumbled.

"What? Some shonky ratbag giving her a hard time?" the Australian said.

I snorted. I didn't know if it was the whiskey or the words "shonky ratbag," but something struck me as mildly hilarious. I took another swallow of my whiskey, still giggling.

"Whoa, Sheila, you're going to be rotten in no time if you keep it up."

"I'm already rotten — that's how I got into this mess," I said.

I suddenly felt very warm. I pulled the sweater over my head and tied it around my waist. The American's eyes bulged as his gaze traveled down my T-shirt and stopped midway. I was too annoyed about everything to care about one stupid ogler. I decided to ignore him. I turned my back to them both and found myself looking at the back of a blond head. He was talking animatedly to another man in a lilting voice. I recognized his profile from the bar at the Dunnery Arms. I was about to open my mouth to say hello when I saw none other than my new friend Richard sitting opposite him.

"Richard!" I yelled, jumping up. I stumbled over the blond and threw my arms around him as if he were a long-lost brother. "I'm s-so happy to s-see you," I said, having some difficulty with the words since the whiskey had numbed my tongue a bit.

Richard graciously let me gush over him, then held me back with a steady hand. "Sweetheart, no offense, but you look like crap. What happened to you?"

"Oh, Richard! Richard!" I said, hanging on his shoulder. "I've soiled his beautiful soul. I've turned Adan into a wanderlust!"

"You've turned him into someone who likes to travel?" Richard asked, looking at me like I was a few shamrocks short of a shake.

"I mean someone who likes to lust. I'm a wanton woman!"

I said the last part loud enough that several heads spun in my direction with raised eyebrows. After taking in my pitiful condition, they apparently decided there wasn't much out of the ordinary to see.

"Doll, we need to get you another drink," Richard said, flagging down the bartender. "Coffee, please. Black."

Good old Richard. "Oh, Richard, what have I done? I've created a mons-s-ster."

226

"What are you talking about, Ren?" Richard said with a seemingly unending well of patience, in spite of the cute blond who kept looking at me as if he wanted me to crawl back under the limestone slab from which I'd come. Richard handed me the coffee and I tried to swallow a few drops, but my hands were shaking.

"Adan —" I started to say, then broke off with a short sob.

"Come on, sweetheart, don't you start crying. Whatever it is I'm sure will work out. There are lots of fish in the sea, my friend. Oh! That reminds me, some guy named Mo has been calling for you, like a trillion times, at the Manor. I was there this morning for golf, and I brought the messages back with me. Actually, it was the same message every time." He reached into his baggy pants and pulled out a small slip of the Manor's stationery. I blinked at it, not quite comprehending.

"Want me to read it to you, doll?" Richard kindly offered.

I nodded morosely, tears still stuck to my inner lashes.

"It says: 'He knows. Andy gave you away. Mo.' That's it. Same message every time, and you're supposed to call him back when you get the message."

I stared at Richard holding the paper, unseeing. Had I heard him right? Did I understand him, or was the whiskey playing tricks with me. *He knows?* As in, he *has* known? That's what Mo was trying to tell me before I left? I'd forgotten about that! I wondered vaguely how long he had known. A great weight that had been bogging me down was slowly lifting from my chest. He knows! This was great news. This meant that he was just . . . Wait a minute. He was just playing with me? Making fun of me? Taunting me?

"Uh, Ren? You're not looking so hot."

Hot was just what I was starting to feel, burning anger from the pit of my stomach. I had a mind to storm back over to the bed-and-breakfast and let Adan have a taste of the sharp tongue I'd been cultivating through years of venomous altercations with senior managers. I must have been scowling at thin air because Richard waved his hand slowly in front of my face.

"Honestly, you can be such a space case, Ren. If you stand there like that much longer, you're going to scare away my prospects." He winked at the blond.

I barely heard what he was saying. Bizarre ideas started to dart into my mind. Maybe I would seduce Adan after all, and give him the shock of his life, or better yet, maybe I could pick up one of these lonely hearts that were clearly desperate for any sort of love. I surveyed the room with little satisfaction. No one here seemed remotely my type. Besides, if I was honest with myself, I knew I'd never have the nerve for a one-night stand — especially not when my heart was still beating in the little bed-and-breakfast down the road. *Shoot.* How had I gotten myself into this mess? Maybe Adan wasn't to blame after all. I hadn't been honest with him, and if I thought about it, he really had given me many opportunities to tell him. He had even prompted it, searched for it . . . *waited* for it. My head was starting to hurt.

"Don't look so glum, sheila — she'll be apples!" the Aussie said to me, pinching me in the rear as he sashayed by with a bubbly blond hanging onto his shoulder.

"Ouch!" I growled.

"Look, doll," said Richard, "I've got a room booked down the street that I don't plan on using . . . Why sleep when you can party, right? But maybe you should go lie down. You're looking a bit pale, and I don't think I can keep track of you in this chaos."

I looked at Richard appreciatively. "Thanks, Richard. That would be nice, actually. I'll be able to think better in the morning."

"Drink up, sweetheart." Richard guided the mug I was holding to my lips. "I'll walk you over."

I finished my coffee, and Richard looped his arm around me, promising the burly blond that he'd be back in a flash and ordering him not to go anywhere. We then sauntered up the street to his hotel room. It was nice, a little less casual than the bed-and-breakfast, but at this point I'd have been willing to sleep standing up propped in the corner of the bar. It felt like I had drunk two pints of whiskey, rather than two measly shots. The effect was mind-numbing . . . and arm-numbing and leg-numbing . . .

"Here we are, doll." I heard Richard's voice through the fog in my head. He was leading me to a little bed in the middle of the room and drawing the curtains. "Now, if you get a wake-up call around eight-thirty, don't be startled. I made myself an appointment with the matchmaker before I was sure I'd be able to find my own 'type' in these parts. You can tell him I want to cancel, thanks but no thanks . . . Richie's still got it!"

"Matchmaker . . . right," I mumbled with my eyes shut. Now that I was lying down, sleep was coming fast.

"See you in the morning, love. Make

yourself at home," he said. I heard the click of the door behind him.

I had only a few more random thoughts about recent events before I plunged into a dreamless sleep. Adan *knew.* I didn't want to think about this right now. I could think about this tomorrow, when my head was clearer. Tomorrow . . .

A mind-piercing ring rudely awakened me. What was that? Why didn't it stop? I painfully opened my eyes to mere slits and felt a moment of panic. Where was I? Then it slowly started to come back . . . Richard. I had run into Richard last night. He had brought me back to his room to sleep off the residual jet lag and the whiskey. *Ugh.* I felt a wave of nausea build in my stomach. I crawled off the bed toward the bathroom, making it just in time. Never again, I promised myself, splashing cold water onto my face. I looked at my reflection and cringed. My mascara had run down my face. What did Mo find so great about mascara, anyway? It was such an inconvenience during crying jags. My hair looked like a rat's nest. My skin was pale and pinched. Coffee — I needed coffee.

I stumbled back to the bed and reached for the phone to dial room service, but it was already ringing — still ringing from before. Relieved that the sound wasn't coming from inside my own head, I tentatively picked up the receiver. "Hello?" I said weakly.

"Richard James?" a woman's voice said.

Hmm. Richard had a first name for a last name too, just like I did.

"Um, no . . ."

"I'm calling to confirm his ten A.M. appointment with Mr. Dooley."

"Mr. Dooley?"

"The matchmaker," she said very slowly as if speaking to a toddler.

"Um . . . just a moment, please."

The matchmaker. Hadn't Richard said something about a wake-up call for his appointment with the matchmaker? What had it been? Cancel it. That was it. Little Richie was doing just fine, or something like that. "I'm sorry but Richard asked me to —" I started to say. Then inspiration hit me. "— Take his appointment instead."

"And your name is?" the woman asked, unsurprised by the request.

"Ren. Ren Edwards."

"Fine. I'll put you in the book. Please meet Mr. Dooley in the village center at ten o'clock sharp. Thank you." She hung up before I could agree.

Now for that coffee. I ordered a large pot, along with a liter of mineral water and some dry soda bread. They were also kind enough to bring me up a new toothbrush. After draining two cups of coffee and half the water, I dragged myself back into the bathroom and into the shower.

The steamy water opened up my pores and evaporated the last remnants of the whiskey. I felt human again as I wiped a circle of fog from the bathroom mirror. Much better. My cheeks looked almost pink. No hair dryer, so I would have to make do with an air dry. When I finished in the bathroom, I went back into the bedroom and sat on the edge of the bed, looking at my crumpled clothes on the floor.

The jeans I could make do with, but I couldn't bear to put on the T-shirt or sweater, which smelled of tobacco and stale beer. I eyed Richard's suitcase on the valet in the corner. Hadn't he told me to make myself at home? I strode over and peeked inside. To my delight, there were three full outfits in there. He couldn't be staying more than two nights, because I knew he was taking the tour to Bunratty Castle on Wednesday. I sifted through the contents and found a lovely, long-sleeved, black V-neck sweater. I slipped it over my head. Richard was slight in build, so it fit me rather nicely, clinging to my curves. It smelled slightly of fabric softener.

I found my purse and pulled out the dreaded mascara. I was meeting a match-maker, after all — might as well at least try to look my best. I then smeared on some lip gloss and pulled on my shoes. It was 9:45 A.M. I didn't have a key, so I stuffed my sweater and belongings into my oversized purse and wrote Richard a thank you note, explaining the sweater I'd borrowed.

I made it downstairs with ten minutes to spare. Lisdoonvarna was such a small town that I wasn't worried about being late. What I was worried about, all of a sudden, was why in the world I had taken this appoint-ment. I tried to remember what I had been thinking this morning during the time when the wooly edges of a hangover were still coloring my decisions. I guess I had thought about unloading all of my self-imposed woes on the matchmaker to see if he had any inspiring ideas for clearing the way to my happiness, but he wasn't a counselor, was he? I didn't even know what his credentials were. For all I knew, he could be a complete crackpot. I was regretting my decision, but it was clearly too late to cancel without ap-pearing rude, and I didn't think I could handle anymore guilt at the moment.

I made sure the coast was clear before I stepped out into the bright street. There was no Adan to be found, so I nervously exited the inn and veered immediately to the left, toward the village center.

A short man with stark white hair and a ruddy complexion was sitting on a folding chair in the village center, happily greeting passers-by. Most of the people looked as if they had either slept in their clothes, or never been to bed at all the prior night. A few were still gripping warm, flat pints of beer. The man in the chair was wearing a tall, puffy black hat, like the one that the Mad Hatter wore, except that this hat had red felt cut-out hearts sewn onto it. A portion of one of the hearts was loose, and it flopped awkwardly when the man turned his head from side to side. I stubbornly tried to bury the crackpot theory, which threatened to turn me on my heels and back to Richard's hotel room, and instead cleared my voice so that it would sound confident.

"Mr. D-Dooley?" I asked. Darn, it came out cracking anyway.

"Ren Edwards?" he asked, glancing down at a computer printout he was holding in one broad hand.

I nodded, looking around apprehensively

at the small crowd that was gathering to snap souvenir photos of the man. "Is there any way we could meet somewhere more . . . private?"

"Aye, a delicate matter is she? Walk with me to O'Clancy's," he said buoyantly. "There we can have a spot o' privacy."

When he rose from the chair, I was embarrassed to see that he couldn't have been more than a little over five feet tall, even with his hat. I felt like an enormous Amazon walking next to him, but followed him dutifully for the short distance across the street to a dark pub. It was surprisingly crowded for this time of day, but Mr. Dooley managed to find us a quiet booth in the very back. Almost everyone else was crowded up at the bar or spilling out onto the street.

"You're a pretty miss. I'd 'ave no trouble matchin' you," he said, looking me up and down appreciatively.

"Thanks, but to tell you the truth —" *The truth.* The words stung my lips as I felt the hypocrisy of them after all this time. "I'm not looking for a match, per se."

He raised his eyebrows at me (at least I think he did, although the rim of the hat was partially covering his brow) and waited politely for me to continue.

"You see, I came here with a man. He's

really quite a lovely man. That is to say, I think that . . . that . . . *I love him,*" I said, my voice cracking again. "But I've been deceiving him . . . and I've just found out he's been deceiving me in a way too, though it's kind of my fault." The words came in a rush then. I spilled the whole sordid story as Mr. Dooley watched with eyes wide in surprise one moment, then squinting deep in thought the next. When I finished, he looked somehow satisfied and more than a little amused.

"I'm glad you've come to me, miss. I believe I 'ave an idea that just might help. Can you stay out o' sight for the rest o' the day, until about four this afternoon at least?" he asked.

I assured him that I could.

"Are you sure now? It may cause this fellow some strain, you disappearin' like that, if he feels about you the way it sounds he does." He looked at me carefully, giving me a chance to back down.

I winced at his words. The thought of Adan in any pain over me caused sharp jabs to my heart and tightness in my chest. Still, I nodded my agreement.

"Very well, miss, I'll be seein' you at four o'clock in this very pub. Enter through the back door. I'll let my men know to be expectin' you."

I thanked him profusely, though I didn't know what for quite yet, and I slipped out the front door. Richard was just passing by the pub, looking pleased. He smiled broadly when he noticed me.

"Is that my Ralph Lauren? Very nice. I only hope I look that good in it," he said merrily. I was marveling that he didn't look the slightest bit worn from being out all night when his eyes quickly darkened.

"Oh, doll, we need to get you out of here. Adan was causing quite a stir this morning, and he's still roaming the streets looking for you. Do you want to take my car and get out of Dodge?"

"You rented a car?"

Richard rolled his eyes in an exaggerated motion. "How did you think I got here — on the wings of love?"

"I guess I never thought about it. Thanks, but no, I plan on staying until this afternoon at least. I took your appointment with the matchmaker this morning, and he —"

Richard held his hand up to stem my flow of words. "You can tell me about it in the room, sweetheart. I'm not kidding you when I say that, unless you want a scene on your hands, you need to get off the street pronto."

I followed Richard back to his room and

waited with strained patience while he disappeared into the bathroom to clean up. A half hour later, we were both sitting snugly on an antique sofa and sipping giant mugs of coffee when I finally got to finish my story. The coffee was starting to make me a little edgy.

"Interesting," Richard said when I had explained most of the morning's events. "So you have no idea what to expect?"

I shook my head. "Nope, but he sounded convinced that he could help."

"Well, doll, if Dooley says he can help you in love, you can bank on it. He's a legend around these parts. Of course, his long-term track record isn't what one would call spectacular — but then, that's not your problem, is it?"

"So, what exactly was going on with Adan this morning?" I asked timidly. "Why would you think that he'd make a scene?"

Richard emitted a wicked laugh. "Actually, I shouldn't be laughing," he snickered. "The poor man was simply beside himself. Apparently, he noticed you missing at around midnight, when he was having a note sent up to your room."

"But, how do you know — ?"

"You know that blond hunk of love from the bar? He's cousins with the porter boy

240

who lives in your B-and-B. He met us at the pub and gave us the scoop after his shift."

"But that porter looked like he was only about fourteen!" I said, shocked.

"Nineteen! They all have such baby faces. Isn't it darling?" Richard said. "Anyway, when Adan tried to send that note up, Finn — that's the boy — told him you weren't up there anymore."

"Wait a minute. Adan was going to make me sit up there waiting and fretting until midnight?" I said, somewhat huffily.

Richard was shaking his head. "I don't think he ever intended to take advantage of you, doll. The note he was sending apparently said that he had business and wouldn't be coming up. He was going to see you again at breakfast in the morning."

Breakfast? He wasn't going to come up? So he hadn't meant to go through with anything lewd after all. He had just been trying to intimidate me — maybe into telling him the truth? I felt another stab of guilty anxiety. If I didn't get this under control soon, I was going to have to seriously contemplate taking up yoga or something.

"So, after Finn told him you were out in town somewhere, Adan got all 'Rambo

meets Willie Worrywart.' He stormed out of
the place and started combing the streets
for you, questioning everyone who could
still stand up straight, and many who
couldn't, for that matter." Richard snickered
again.

"What?"

"You should have seen him when he ran
across your little Australian and American
friends. They made the mistake of implying
that they'd seen more of you than they
really did, and certainly more than you
would have tolerated — the lanky bonehead
actually admitted that your rear end was
firmer than any he'd felt in the county . . .
Was that him who pinched you just before
we left?"

I stared at Richard unspeaking, horror
etched in my face, and nodded.

"The little creep. Anyway, Adan wasn't
too pleased by their description of their
encounter with you, and when they couldn't
give him any information about your cur-
rent whereabouts, he started a little brawl."

"A brawl?" I said, unbelieving.

"Well, not much of a brawl, to tell you the
truth. One slam of the American's head
against the counter, and he lost his front
tooth and went running off whimpering like
a baby. The Australian was a bit thicker-

242

skinned, but it only took Adan one punch to have him on the floor, moaning that he'd broken his nose."

I couldn't believe it. "Adan got into a brawl over me?" I swallowed hard. "Didn't . . . didn't he see you?" I asked.

"Heck no, sweetheart. I ducked behind the counter until he left. My man is friendly with the proprietors too, so they didn't mind the minor intrusion. I saw and heard the whole thing from where I was crouched three feet off the floor behind the bar."

"What . . . happened to Adan?"

"Well, the proprietor was just summoning the big boys from the back room when Adan put up his hands in surrender. He wasn't looking for a fight — he was just looking for you. They really couldn't blame him — the fight found him all on its own. The proprietor seemed to sympathize with him, with it being matchmaking season and all, and let him off the hook. He did tell Adan that he'd served you at least two whiskeys before he lost track of you. Luckily, he didn't see you leave with me."

"So you think Adan's still out there looking now?" I asked.

"Doll, I know he is. I saw him sitting like a tragic hero on the pavement outside one of the pubs, holding his head in his hands as if he'd committed some unforgivable sin. He did not look well, I tell you."

I glanced over at Richard's watch. It was only one o'clock. How could I let Adan wander the streets for another three hours in such torment? I couldn't. I had to go find him. "I have to go find him," I faltered, standing up.

"What? Come on, sweetheart, where's your resolve? It won't be long now."

"No." I shook my head. "I'm done playing games. I'm the one that started this and should have finished it a long time ago. I can't do this any longer — can't bring Adan this kind of pain. I . . . I love him too much." My voice broke pathetically, and I started to cry as the last words barely squeaked out.

When I looked at Richard, he had tears in his eyes and was blowing his nose loudly into a napkin leftover from the breakfast service.

"You go get him, sweetheart!" he said, jumping up to hold open the door for me.

I didn't waste any time bounding down the stairs, nearly bowling over several people just turning in from the prior night's festivities. I bolted out the front door and into the street, ignoring stares of curiosity from the proprietors. Desperately, I craned my neck to look down each street. The streets were emptier now, as people were catching a few hours of sleep before the partying started again at four. I didn't see anyone of Adan's stature anywhere in sight. My heart strained painfully in my chest.

I decided to circle the village once so that I could clearly look down all the streets. Then, if I didn't find him, I would systematically start checking each of the pubs and restaurants, starting from the far end of the street. I assumed Adan would be making his way in this direction.

To my chagrin, I had no luck with the streets. He was nowhere to be found. I had questioned a few bleary-eyed people stumbling back to their hotels, but nothing. Some of the girls had said that they'd noticed a very good-looking, but surly-faced man combing the town, but when he'd ignored their flirting, they'd given up. No one had any idea where he was now. Frustrated, I stepped into the first pub to continue my search.

I received no satisfaction from the proprietor or from any of the patrons who were now beginning to fill the pubs again. The kindly barkeeper's face did light up when she made the connection that *I* was the young woman that the poor bloke had been searching for all morning, but she hadn't a clue as to where he'd gone off to next.

The thickening crowds were making my mission more and more difficult. Every time I caught the back of a black-haired head, I was heartily disappointed to see that it was just some stranger enjoying the party. In my frantic anticipation, I began to see Adan's face everywhere, only to be crushed by disappointment again and again. I was depressed and weary when I finally reached the pub in which I had agreed to meet Mr. Dooley.

I glanced at the large round clock on the wall. It was now almost four in the afternoon. I had been searching for almost three hours. I thought of the matchmaker. Could he really do anything for me? I was truly desperate to find out. I exited the pub's front entrance and made my way down the alley beside it. When I got to the back, I nodded solemnly at two bulky men smoking clove cigarettes in front of the door. They nodded, and I slipped into the back entrance.

It was dark in the narrow hallway, especially after the bright sunlight of the streets. I could still smell the sweet scent of cloves lingering in the air. A young woman with blond, curly hair emerged from the shadows and tugged urgently at my arm as if she had been expecting me. I followed her through an ever-narrower hallway, up three steps to a small space behind a heavy curtain. I looked at her questioningly, but she held up her hand indicating that I should be silent and wait.

I could hear Mr. Dooley's voice, boisterous and booming, on the other side of the curtain. He was a small man, but he made up for it with the power in his voice.

"Young misses and gents, I welcome ye to the final week of the annual Lisdoonvarna Matchmakin' Festival!"

Roars of applause and laughter met his introduction. How many people were out there anyway?

"I've made many a happy match o'er the years, and it warms me heart like the cracklin' fire from me own mother's kitchen," he said to more rowdy applause.

The people seemed to love his contrived accent.

"As ye know, the grand finale of the festivities is only a few wee days away."

More cheering and catcalls.

"Then I'll be namin' the long-anticipated Queen of the Burren and Mr. Lisdoonvarna."

The crowd went wild, whistling and shouting.

"But before that, I have a very special couple to announce . . ."

I felt my stomach do a flip as I listened, partly in fear, partly in wild hopefulness.

"Today I will award one special couple to be Mr. and Miss Most-Eligible-to-Love."

The crowd could barely contain their excitement. Someone began banging a table with their mug in a rhythm that the rest of the crowd quickly picked up with their own beers or by stomping their feet.

" 'Most Eligible' because this couple is truly worthy of bein' chosen. They just don't know it yet."

A wave of good-humored laughter rose from the crowd.

"They are perfectly suited to one another. Unbeknownst to each other, each has come to me independently this morning, layin' open a pained and broken heart."

More subdued laughter now, a tone of understanding.

My ears pricked and my heart seemed to freeze in place in my chest. *What had he just said?*

"Each half of this couple may have been tellin' their own little white lie, but only out of fear of never knowin' what it is to be loved for their true self by the other. Each of them has a heart that rings true . . . as true as our lovely vale runs wide."

An excited murmur now ran through the crowd.

"This couple has been impossibly separated for too long, and now they are to be impossibly reconnected. In love, all things are possible, my friends. Ye would do well to remember that!"

More raucous applause.

"This couple, they are indeed a match made in heaven itself. Please join me in welcomin' to our little stage, Mr. and Miss Most-Eligible-to-Love: *Mr. Adan Bennett and Miss Ren Edwards!*"

A deafening roar surfaced from behind the curtain. I felt myself being shoved through the slits and out into the open by the thin, white arms of the red-haired woman who had been standing next to me. I squinted against a bright light that was shining up on the stage. I lifted my hand to shield my eyes. My heart was thumping wildly in my chest now. I could see that someone was being shoved with vigor from the front of the room through the thick crowd toward the back stage.

My heart stopped mid-beat, then leapt. *It was Adan!* He looked as stunned as I felt, and even more anxious. But when he met and locked gazes with me from across the distance, his face registered both immense relief and heavy remorse.

I didn't wait for him to reach the stage. I sprang down and started winding my way through the parting crowd. Everyone around us was screaming, jumping and raising their mugs in a celebratory toast. When I met Adan in the center of the room, I hesitated. Now that I was standing in front of him, my courage was waning. Would he be furious with me for lying to him? Would he he understand I'd had to do it . . . for my job?

Adan also seemed hesitant to reach out to me, but the crowds cheered us on. I took a large gulp of air and threw myself at him, to the great pleasure of the crowd. Adan instinctively caught me against his strong chest and wrapped his arms around my waist, clenching me to him. I stood on my tiptoes to speak into his ear, and he responded by bending his head closer so he could hear me. "I never meant to hurt you," I said, tears edging into my voice. "I just — I . . ."

Adan pulled my face into his chest, embracing me tightly, as if I might vaporize if he released me. He buried his face in my

hair. I could hear his jagged breath, sounding gravely relieved.

"I thought I'd lost you for good," he said,
his low voice catching in pain.

As soon as we'd embraced each other, the
crowd seemed sufficiently satisfied with our
reunion that they had gone back to their
partying. This left us with relative privacy in
the midst of the crowd. I could see Mr.
Dooley beam at us from the stage before he
descended and joined the party. He gave us
a joyful little wave. I waved back shyly, then
looked up at Adan.

"I should have told you. I never should
have . . ."

Adan held his finger gently to my lips.
"Shhh," he whispered. Then he bent his
head even closer to mine and closed the gap
with such a passionate kiss that it felt like
the ends of my hair would burst into flames.
Everything in the room faded away, and
time stood still. I could hear only the beating of my heart against Adan's and his
rough breathing as his lips melted over
mine.

Then he pulled away, scooped me up with
one grand gesture and sailed through the
crowd, out the front door. He put me down
in the street, wordlessly took my hand and
led me back toward the bed-and-breakfast.

Now that we were away from the crowd and his lips were no longer scrambling my brain, I could think a bit more clearly. I felt like I needed to explain.

"Adan —" I started. "I never meant to lie to you . . . Pretending to be married is part of my role, for my job . . . and when I met you I had no idea that I was going to fall in love with you . . ."

Adan stopped abruptly and smiled so adoringly that I thought my knees would collapse from beneath me.

"You love me?" he asked, eyes glinting warmly.

I thought that he was missing my point. "My job . . . It's to —"

"You *really* love me?" he interrupted, thoroughly unconcerned with the rest of my explanation.

"Well . . . yes," I said, my voice breaking with emotion.

"Hmm," he said thoughtfully. The sound sizzled.

His response left me more than a little confused and dazed. I didn't attempt any further explanation as he turned away from me, still smiling, and unlocked the door leading to our room. He turned back to me, circling his arms around my waist, and I tilted my face toward his. I let my head drop back and closed my eyes, anticipating the kiss.

It didn't come.

I opened my eyes to peek, and I noticed Adan looking at me with a bemused expression.

"What is it?" I managed to say.

"Ren?" he said, his voice low and sensuous, better than in my very best dreams.

I nodded feebly, completely in his power.

"Will you go to England with me? Just the two of us?"

My eyes flew open now, wide and alert. He looked a little alarmed by my response.

"Go to England?" I asked.

"Yes, stay with me after the tour group goes back and we can travel to England together. I'd like you to see my old stomping grounds . . . and to meet my father."

My voice was a hoarse, confused whisper. "W-why?"

"Because I want to be with you, Alizarin Crimson Edwards . . . *Ren, I love you.*"

My blood pulsed through my body and pooled in my ears as he said those magical words.

"I've wanted you from the first time I saw you in that silly bathrobe, eating lunch at the spa. It was torturous, trying to keep away from you and cursing the fact that you were married, that I was too late."

I balked, embarrassed. "Be serious."

"I am very serious. Would it help if I knelt down? I can't bear to be without you . . . Please, stay with me."

"I-I don't know what to say." He wanted me. I smiled faintly, unable to quite fathom that I deserved this much happiness.

A sly smile played at Adan's lips. "Say yes. Really, Ren, I can't go all my life waiting to catch you between husbands."

I tilted my head back and laughed softly, remembering one of my favorite scenes from *Gone with the Wind,* but the sound caught in my throat as Adan's lips found my pulse there and silenced me. His lips traveled slowly back to my mouth.

"Tell me you'll stay," he said softly against my lips.

I felt drunk with longing.

"I . . . I can't think clearly."

"You don't have to — just *say* you'll stay . . ." His teasing lips moved from mine to the sweet spot just below my ear. My eyes fluttered shut.

"Say it . . . ," he purred.

"Yes! Yes! I'll stay," I said, on one breath. I was sure my boss would understand. Maybe he'd even chalk it up to another "experience."

I felt Adan's lips spread into a grin, and I momentarily mourned the loss of them against my neck.

"You aren't just saying that to get me to stop?" he asked, his voice husky.

"No . . . ," I said, my voice sounding like a whimper.

He cocked an eyebrow at me.

"But, yes, you *should* stop."

Adan kissed me full on the mouth before lifting his head and pulling reluctantly away. He stepped back over the threshold and into the hall.

"I've booked another room two doors down. I'm going to get cleaned up and meet you downstairs in an hour."

"A whole hour?" I hated the idea of spending any time away from Adan now that everything was out in the open.

"If it's okay with you, I'd like to take you to dinner and to watch the fireworks. Then tomorrow, there's a few archaeological sites off the beaten path I'd love to show you."

I nodded. The way I felt about Adan, something told me the fireworks I saw that evening would have nothing to do with the matchmaking festival.

Well, almost nothing.

EPILOGUE

Mo looked at me slyly from across the table, then threw back another vodka tonic.

"Got any more fives?" she shouted over the deafening pulse of the dance music.

I shook my head stubbornly and diverted my eyes, as I'd been trying to do all night; still, it was impossible to completely ignore the bronze dancer who was suggestively wiggling his scantily clad body near our front-row table. All of the other ladies with us were definitely getting into the moment, waving dollar bills and shaking their own bodies to the rhythm.

"I can*not* believe I let you talk me into this!" I said through gritted teeth.

"Oh relax — we haven't even come to the best part yet."

"I shudder to think," I said flatly.

The earlier part of the evening had gone pretty much as I had expected with lots of female friends and colleagues who had joined us at an upscale bar. They had showered me with dainty lingerie, something I would finally get to use now that I was getting married. Then Mo had had the brilliant idea to drag us off to this seedy little joint where I'd been horrified to look anywhere but into my purse or at Mo since I'd arrived. Even the waiter had startled me, wearing nothing but tight black shorts and a bow tie.

"Here it comes," Mo said, barely able to contain her excitement.

I heard the bass soften and the music shift from Euro-trash to an almost-obscene version of the wedding march. I groaned in protest.

"Oh no, Mo, *no!* Tell me you didn't —"

"Honey, you only get married once. Well, that may not be true, but for you, I'm sure it is." She grinned wickedly. "Watch the show — you'll like this. I promise," she insisted.

I reluctantly lifted my eyes to the stage. No one was there, but someone had rolled a giant papier-mâché, five-tiered wedding cake into the middle of it.

"Oh no," I repeated.

"Oh yes," Mo said.

Just then the music shifted back to club music, and a man popped out of the top of the cake. The ladies around me whooped and hollered. Mo was laughing hysterically, for some reason that had not yet struck me. I took one glance at the tiny bottoms he was wearing and flushed redder than my name, and then my eyes darted away. I'd just have to try to concentrate on his face.

His face! I couldn't believe it. Now I understood Mo's hysterics. It was none other than *Andy*. Andy was at my bachelorette party, pumping to the groove for our entertainment! I'm sure he didn't realize yet that I was supposed to be the target of attention, so focused was he on squeezing his eyes shut with his hands behind his head and moving his hips to the rhythm. I threw my hand over my open mouth, and the sound that escaped was a high squeak, followed by a riotous laugh.

The sound caught Andy's attention and he jiggled over, obviously intending to delight us with his dancing, but when he saw me clearly, his own jaw dropped and he turned white. He spent the rest of the song on the opposite end of the stage, shaking his booty at some more enthusiastic ladies nearer the bar.

"Did you actually arrange that?" I asked Mo later that evening.

"Well, I didn't hire him specifically if

that's what you mean. But I had heard that he was moonlighting here after his divorce became final. It was his ex-wife that made all the real money in their household, so he was pretty desperate when she got fed up and left him."

"Well, good for her," I said, smugly.

"Though I have to say, he looked like he was enjoying that a little too much."

"Mm-hmm," I agreed, musing about how people always seem to get what they deserve in the end, and realizing that I was no exception. And that thought comforted me greatly.

The employees of Thorndike Press hope you have enjoyed this Large Print book. All our Thorndike, Wheeler, and Kennebec Large Print titles are designed for easy reading, and all our books are made to last. Other Thorndike Press Large Print books are available at your library, through selected bookstores, or directly from us.

For information about titles, please call:
  (800) 223-1244

or visit our Web site at:
  http://gale.cengage.com/thorndike

To share your comments, please write:
  Publisher
  Thorndike Press
  295 Kennedy Memorial Drive
  Waterville, ME 04901

ME   8/10